Scribbler of Dreams

Scribbler of Dreams

MARY E. PEARSON

Harcourt, Inc.

San Diego   New York   London

www.harcourt.com

Library of Congress Cataloging-in-Publication Data
Pearson, Mary (Mary E.)
Scribbler of dreams/by Mary E. Pearson.
p. cm.
Summary: Despite her family's long feud with the Crutchfields,
seventeen-year-old Kaitlin falls in love with Bram Crutchfield and
weaves a tangled web of deception to conceal her identity from him.
[1. Vendetta—Fiction. 2. Honesty—Fiction. 3. Love—Fiction.]
I. Title.
PZ7.P32316Sc 2001
[Fic]—dc21 00-11342
ISBN 0-15-202320-8

Text set in Dante
Designed by Lydia D'moch

First edition
A C E G H F D B
Printed in the United States of America

For Karen and Jessica,
with my love

If we could read the secret history of our enemies,
we should find in each man's life
sorrow and suffering enough to disarm all hostility.

—*Henry Wadsworth Longfellow*

Chapter 1

"I HATE THE CRUTCHFIELDS!"

I had always hated the Crutchfields.

I was born to hate the Crutchfields.

I glanced from the mirror to my open bedroom door, hoping my mother hadn't heard me. Today was as hard for her as it was for me. Maybe harder.

She poked her head in the door. She'd heard.

"Almost ready?" she asked.

"Two more minutes," I said. I tried to sound perky. Perky. Right. "Tell Abby to wait in the car for me."

My mom sighed. "Kaitlin—"

"No, Mom. Don't start. It's only a school. Relax. Everything will be fine."

She nodded and left.

But everything wasn't fine. It would never be fine again. I was about to start my senior year at a Crutchfield school. On Crutchfield land. Bought with Crutchfield money. Probably only whores went there. My parents had sacrificed for years to send me and my sister to a private Christian school. Not that they were religious, but they would sooner die than see their kids in a school built on Crutchfield land. My father didn't know yet. We couldn't tell him. Not with everything he had been through... everything the Crutchfields had done to him.

The hate my family had nursed for generations was no longer a casual fact in my head. I felt it. I wanted it. It burned inside of me. It was something I could count on, when I could count on nothing else.

I took a last look in my cracked dresser mirror and pulled my long, dark hair into a ponytail. I twisted it into a bun and tucked my T-shirt into my jeans. It didn't help.

"You'll never fit in, Kaitlin Malone," I whispered. I opened my eyes wide so tears couldn't gather and spill down my cheeks. There was no time for that.

"Kait! Hurry up!"

The screen door squeaked, followed by its familiar bang. The only thing worse than going to Twin Oaks High School was going there with my sister. Thank God she was a freshman and, hopefully, I would never see her.

"Coming!" I yelled back. I grabbed my journal from my dresser and read my last entry.

September 6.
Back and forth. Back and forth. The tide ebbs and
swirls, surrounding, reaching, touching with its foamy
fingers. Teasing at my last breathless moments. Surging
up and over, pulling me under. The tide is winning...

I added a few more words.

...but for a moment my foot brushes the bottom, and I
am able to push, to grasp hold of a few last breaths. For
a moment the tide must wait.

I threw the journal into my backpack and grabbed an
apple from the kitchen counter as I ran out the door.
Abby had grabbed my keys and already started the car.
She had turned up the radio so it blared. As I slid into the
driver's seat, my mom ran out the back door and down
our sagging wooden steps. I reached over and turned the
radio off. Abby glared at me, as if I cared.

My mom bent over and motioned for me to roll the
window down. She just couldn't let go. To her, more
words were like a stay of execution, but they just made
my heart pound faster.

"Kaitlin, I know you will make ... the best of it. Watch
out for your sister. Okay? Stick together. The Malones always stick together. And try not to spend all your free
time with your nose stuck in your journal. Make friends."
Friends? My mom was delusional. She waited for me to
respond. Her eyes glistened and an anxious smile was
frozen across her face. It was pitiful.

I hated the Crutchfields. For everything they had done.

I nodded to reassure her and even said I would keep an eye out for Abby. A lie. But I knew it made her feel better. She turned and walked back to the house, but then stopped a few steps away and whirled back around. "And remember! Kaitlin and Abby *Hampton*. Hampton. And it's not a lie—not really—you are Hamptons, too. Remember that. It will just make things . . . easier. Right?"

But it was a lie, no matter how you worded it. I didn't answer her. I couldn't. It seemed like the final, ultimate betrayal, but as my mom had explained—it would make things "easier." Easier compared to what? Easier compared to the living hell we had already been through? I wondered sometimes what a "normal" life would feel like. More than wondered. I yearned for it . . . to simply be seventeen and only worry about grades, dances, clothes . . . boys. *Is* that what normal seventeen-year-olds worried about? I didn't know.

Abby leaned across my lap and yelled out the window. "Yes! Hampton! We got it, Mom! Gotta go!" She tapped on the horn twice like she was issuing the final dismissal. I put the car in gear. Abby didn't mind being registered at school under our mom's maiden name. She had been using it all summer, in fact, since she joined the freshman soccer team. She had left Malone behind her like yesterday's dirty socks, waiting for a good washing before putting them on again. But a name is not like socks. Tossing it aside will not change who you are. I am a Malone. Period. Even if my school records now say Hampton.

4

When I circled around on the dirt drive, I could see the bobbing heads of workers as they picked tomatoes in our fields. White, then blue, then tan. Their covered heads went up and down in a comforting rhythm. Some things didn't change. The harvest had been good so far. We were all hoping it would be a miracle season. A long season. A bountiful crop with high prices. *Please let it be a good season.* We needed the money. Bad. The attorney's fees to defend my father had eaten up all of our savings.

Two years ago the crop had been good. My dad said we even had enough left over to fix up the house a bit. God knows, the monster needed it. The roof leaked. The white paint was blistering off like dandruff. The sagging porch threatened to collapse at any moment. But there was no money now for fixing anything.

When my dad killed Robert Crutchfield eighteen months ago, everything changed.

"So *you* are going to keep an eye on *me?*" Abby asked as we bumped along toward the main road.

It *was* a ridiculous thought. Abby was the one who had friends at the high school. Girls from her soccer team. Boys she met at the mall. Anyone who would listen to her prattle. Abby was not shy.

"I have no intention of keeping an eye on you. I have better things to do."

"Like what? Scribble in your stupid journal? I hope you take Mom's advice and try to make friends. I don't want the whole world to think my sister is some kind of loser."

"Well, I certainly wouldn't want to damage your reputation by acting halfway literate—oh, excuse me. That's too big of a word for you to understand, isn't it?"

Abby shut up, but I almost missed the banter. It distracted me from the wild dance going on in my stomach.

I searched for the hate that had stiffened my spine moments earlier, the hate that put an angry furrow across my brow, like my grandmother's. I thought about the Crutchfields. I tried to fan the embers, to feel the glowing coal of hate, the coal that would chase away the icy grip of fear growing inside me. But with each mile we traveled, I could only think of how alone I felt. The fear was winning. Winding its way past my stomach, through my veins, its cold fingers tightening their hold on my chest.

I pushed against the sand, a breath, one more breath.

I *was* a Malone. I would make the best of it.

Chapter 2

BEFORE I COULD EVEN put the car in park, Abby was bounding out the door. I can't say I blamed her. Our rusty Buick rumbled into the parking lot like some ancient steam engine, and it coughed and rattled long after I had turned the motor off. A stark contrast to the shiny Jeeps and Beemers that sparkled in neat rows. Twin Oaks was so preppy, it was pathetic.

"Abby! Wait!" I called. "Don't forget that you take the bus home! Do you know which one to take?"

She mumbled something and waved as she ran off, which I assumed meant that she would be okay. But what about me? I had refused to go to orientation with Abby, thinking there might be a reprieve from this whole ordeal, but the reprieve didn't come, and now I had to find my way around this sprawling campus. I pulled my crumpled schedule and a map from my backpack.

1	AP Eng	Rm 510	Perez
2	AP Calc	Rm 212	Greer
3	AP Bio	Rm 16B	Shidrowski
4	AP Govt	Rm 824	Bailey
	Lunch		
5	Srvy Hist/Cul	Rm 520	Ames

I only had to take five classes because I already had so many credits. One class after lunch, and I was out of here. That was why Abby had to take the bus, but I knew she didn't mind. She would rather yak with her friends than with me.

I turned the map around trying to make sense of it. There didn't seem to be any reasoning to the numbering of buildings. There were so many. I couldn't even find the 500s on the map. Holy Trinity Academy was never like this. I missed its smallness.

Students rushed past me, all confident of where they were going. Nearly three thousand of them. How could a school be so big? I joined the swarm, pushed along in the current of chattering faces. But none chattered with me. I might as well have been faceless. I searched for numbers on the sides of buildings, but there were none. A knot grew in my throat as the crowds thinned. A rapid flutter beat against my chest. They all seemed to be finding their classes, except me. I studied the map again.

Brrring!

I looked up. The halls, the lawns—they were all empty.

God, what was I doing here! I hated this school. I hated the Crutchfields. I fought the panic rising in me. I resisted my muscles, already quickening, testing, ready to sprint to my car, to run from everything before it was too late.

I jumped at a tap on my shoulder and spun around.

"Let's have a look." A human being was actually speaking to me and reaching for my schedule. "Five-ten. Right behind you. It's that room right there." The woman smiled and handed my schedule back to me.

"Thank you," I mumbled. I thought the worst was behind me, but when I walked into the already seated classroom, every eye turned. Bore into me. Scrutinized the way I walked, the way I wore my hair, the way I clumsily slid into the only empty seat. The way I fumbled for a pencil. The way I tried to sit up straight, tried to slouch, tried to be invisible.

Every class was the same. I was the outsider—the one who was different from everyone else. I cringed each time the teacher would call roll—would announce that Kaitlin Hampton occupied a seat in the classroom. Daughter of a Crutchfield killer. But no one noticed because Hampton was not a name that had splashed the nightly news for endless months. Mother's plan was working. It didn't bring me comfort.

It seemed that throughout the day I was dropping pencils, sitting in the wrong seat, or passing papers in the wrong direction. I was not one of them. I would never be.

I was out of step with the finely tuned machine of students who knew one another, had worked with one another, had told secrets with one another for years. When the bell rang after fourth period, I was the first one out of the room. I breathed in deeply, like I had been struggling underwater for hours.

I had only taken a few steps outside when I heard a whistle and a "Yeah!" I turned and two boys who looked like bookends—black shorts, white T-shirts, hats on backward—were grinning at me. My face burned and I felt a wave of heat rush across my chest. My mind raced. Were they flirting? Making fun of me? I didn't know. God, I was out of step. I awkwardly turned and hurried away. I had to find a quiet place. A place to be alone and think.

I couldn't go sit in my car. The September sun was already making the black asphalt parking lot squiggle back and forth with waves of heat. I started down a walkway, not knowing where it would take me. I only knew it was the opposite direction of where most students seemed to be walking. Groups of laughing girls bumped into me as they passed. I was a nonevent, the bump unnoticed, not even worthy of a turned head. I watched them casually toss their heads back as relaxed laughter tumbled past their perfect white teeth. They looked shallow, self-absorbed. And a small, strangled part of me envied them.

On the far side of the campus, I found a secluded, shady courtyard that bordered a grassy knoll and I sat down on a brick planter. I was as far from the chaos of the noisy lunch lines and strolling crowds as I could possibly be—and I was alone. Perfect.

I briefly thought about my mom and Abby's advice, but they didn't understand. Writing in my journal—it gave a place for all the words and feelings that bounced around in my head.

A fear...a dream—often nothing at all—but a glimpse, a shadow of something fleeting past my consciousness, something I can't grasp with my mind but I can slow it down, bring it into focus if I ease the words across paper. Some people play soccer, some people jog, why shouldn't I "scribble," as Abby puts it? I pulled my journal from my backpack, along with my apple and a bottle of water. I closed my eyes. It was silent, except for the occasional chirp of a sparrow or the distant shout of friends calling to each other. The warm summer air held me. My pounding heart quieted. My shoulders dropped, relaxed, and I opened my eyes to write.

My half-opened lids shot open wide, and I sat up straight, clutching my journal to my chest. I wasn't alone anymore. Twenty feet from me on the grassy knoll, beneath the shade of a tree, a boy was lying down. He rested his head on a backpack and his eyes were closed. Why was he way over here? No friends, either? An outcast? I couldn't see much of his face, but his straight blond hair was slicked back and was clumped into thick strands. His clothes were uneventful—like mine. Old blue jeans and a plain white T-shirt.

I stared at him for a long while. He didn't move. I

could barely see his chest rise and fall, and I decided his peaceful slumber wouldn't bother me. I would share this quiet corner with him. I picked up my journal and began to write. As each word spilled out, I felt the tension leave my shoulders, my neck, my soul. The world around me became a blur as I tried to give it order.

Green. Brown. Green. Brown. Row after row of dark earth and robust plants, carrying the hope of tomorrow in their red fruit. Hope that there would be a tomorrow. Their roots reaching down, sucking every drop of water, holding on to every grain of soil. Holding on . . .

I set my journal aside and breathed deeply, stretching my arms overhead.

I jerked my hands back to my lap—the boy had sat up. He was writing, too. I watched his broad strokes and realized he wasn't writing but sketching. Maybe the tree he sat under or the surrounding buildings. The look on his face was how I imagined I must look when I write in my journal. Oblivious to everything but still purposeful, intense. Perhaps not all the boys at Twin Oaks were like the mindless bookends I had encountered.

Some laughter and hoots drew my attention to the walkway. A group of three girls and two boys approached.

"Bram! My man!" one of the boys shouted as the group tromped across the grass and exchanged slaps and handshakes with the boy sitting beneath the tree.

"Bram," I whispered. *So his name is Bram.* Different.

And he did have friends. The group continued on their way and Bram went back to his sketching, but a few minutes later the whole scene was repeated with another group. They fussed over him, like he was a king.

He had friends all right—a lot of friends.

With the second group gone, the peace of the courtyard returned. Bram continued with his sketching, and I wondered about this popular boy who sought the solitude of an isolated courtyard. Why? I hadn't even realized I was staring, until he looked up, straight at me. I caught my breath. Even at twenty feet I could see the intensity of his icy blue eyes. One, two, three seconds the stare continued. I was mortified that I didn't look away first. He looked back down and resumed his sketching, but I could still feel his piercing blue eyes. I felt the burning flush that plagued me rush across my cheeks.

Brrring!

Lunch was over. Thank God. I gathered up my stuff and hurried away, still feeling the blush on my face. Only one more hour of this wretched Crutchfield school.

My last class, Survey of Local History and Culture, was a joke. A graduation requirement, a complete waste of my time, and a final slap in my face by the Crutchfields. A reminder that I was in a place I didn't want to be. I sat through it in a daze, and when the bell finally rang, I rushed out to the parking lot. Since most students still had a sixth period, the lot was full of cars but nearly empty of students.

I paused near my car and looked back at the buildings.

Acres of concrete surrounded by more acres of concrete, as far as the eye could see. It wasn't always that way. But that was the Crutchfields' specialty. Change.

I got in my car and rolled down the windows. I sped off, letting the wind blow wildly through the car. Letting it blow all memories of the day away. Letting it blow all thoughts, period, from my mind.

But the wind couldn't blow away the memory of an icy blue gaze.

Chapter 3

A CLOUD OF DUST billowed behind me as I turned at the fork in our road and headed for the Malone Company offices. It was nothing more than a rambling tin hut that looked out over our fields. It was partitioned off into three sections. One office for payroll and billing, my mom's job. One office for ordering and shipping and overall supervision, now my mom's job, too. And a third office for our foreman. He supervised the planting, spraying, and harvesting of the crops. He was a new man. I didn't care for him, but I knew we were lucky to have him. José, our foreman for as long as I can remember, had a heart attack and had to retire. It was shortly after we lost my dad, so my mom was grateful that someone with experience answered her ad. She could take over my dad's job for a while, but not the foreman's, too.

I opened the door and let the spring slam it behind me. Rick, the foreman, was sitting with his feet up on his desk, smoking a cigarette.

"Hi, Rick. Have you seen my mom?"

"She left early. Went down to San Diego," he said in his gravelly voice. He sat up and looked at me, his head slightly tilted and his eyes squinting, like he was trying to see inside my brain.

I tried to act unaffected, but I knew what going to San Diego meant. She had gone to see my dad. I opened my mouth to change the subject, but Rick went on.

"She's an awful pretty lady to be goin' through all this. I think—"

"Thanks, Rick. I'll see her later at home."

I stumbled back through the door and leaned against the wavy sides of the hut, hoping Rick hadn't seen my glistening eyes. The hot metal wall burned against my skin, but mostly I felt the hot stinging tears running down my cheeks. I didn't need an outsider like Rick to tell me what my mother was going through. I pushed away from the wall and walked up the hill—to the section of fields that looked out to the ocean and beyond. I headed for "my rock," a large flat boulder that had always been my refuge as a child. It had served as a castle, an island, a tree house—whatever my imagination needed it to be that day. Today I just needed it to be far away from everything else.

My tears turned to anger, fueling my pace up the hill.

By the time I reached the crest, I had to lean over on my knees to catch my breath. The lump in my throat was cutting off my air. I closed my eyes and forced the air in, slowly, deeply. I wiped my eyes and straightened up.

I was a small speck, alone, on top of the world. That's all I wanted to be ... surrounded by the precious acres of Malone land, the sprawl of Twin Oaks, the expanse of the Pacific Ocean. I was ten years old again and invincible. Why did things have to change?

Why did my father have to kill a Crutchfield?

It was an accident, of course. But who would believe it? The hatred between the Crutchfields and the Malones goes back five generations, when the Crutchfield sisters first parted ways.

Maggie Crutchfield was a slut. She slept around with anything that wore pants. When she became pregnant without the benefit of marriage, her sister, Amanda Crutchfield Malone, refused to see her ever again. When their parents died and left them the thousands of acres that is now Twin Oaks, they divided the land down the middle. An ancient barbed-wire fence still marks the division in some places.

Views were a dime a dozen back then, so not much thought was given to that when dividing up the land, but the Malones got the best of it. I am grateful for that every time I escape to my rock. From hilltop after hilltop we can see the ocean and beyond. We know that sticks in the Crutchfields' throats like a splintered chicken bone— million-dollar views being wasted on tomatoes. Not that they would ever enjoy a view. Maggie Crutchfield exploited her share of the Crutchfield inheritance. She sold off huge chunks, shamelessly developed other parts, and—when it suited her purpose—she plain gave it away. My parents say it was the only way a woman like her could gain any acceptance in her day. Even the biggest prude will look the other way when a slut donates money. There is hardly an acre of Crutchfield land now that doesn't have a hotel, shopping center, or housing tract on it. They are filthy rich. My parents always emphasize the filthy part.

Their greedy empire blends in with the suburban sprawl that spreads for miles and miles, while the Malone land is a green jewel, a breathing space, a quirky wonder in the sea of concrete. Not one acre—not one—has ever been sold.

It is the pride of the Malones, but it also means we are usually broke.

I've heard the story a thousand times. My grandmother used to tell it before she died, and now my father carries on the tradition—or at least he did. The Crutchfields are not to be trusted. They have no feelings. No sense of right or wrong. Empty shells that devour everything in their path. It is how they have always been—how they will always be. It has always bonded the Malones, as few as we are, knowing it is us against them. It was hard to believe we were related to the Crutchfields.

I saw a trail of dust move along on the road far below me. It was my mom. I wondered what part of her would be gone today. What part of her spirit would be expertly dissected and removed by a system that kept her from her husband of twenty years. She and my dad were very close, and each time she came back from visiting him she looked a little more tired, a little older. They sentenced my mother to prison as surely as they had sentenced my dad, except she still had a farm to run and daughters to raise.

My eyes wandered past the trail of billowing dust to the Crutchfield empire beyond. They had no idea how much pain their lies had caused. But someday they would know. I would make sure of that.

I ran down the hill to my Buick and drove home.

MY MOM WAS in her bedroom when I got there—with the door closed. I knew what that meant, too. Soon I would hear the shower pipes clanging, and then later she would emerge as though the water could wash away the pain. It could at least hide her tears. She was a Malone, too, making the best of it.

I ran up the stairs and flopped on my bed. I wanted to call Becky Miller, my best friend at Holy Trinity Academy, but I was afraid if she started telling me about her first day, I might cry. I didn't want to cry anymore. Instead, I pulled all the papers from my backpack that my mom had to sign. Contracts that I would arrive on time, turn my homework in, respect others, complete all assignments—that I wouldn't cheat! What a waste of paper. I skimmed through the syllabus from my biology class, then my

English class. It wasn't what I expected. All my years at Holy Trinity, I imagined that "the other school" would be as shallow as the Crutchfields. These classes actually looked like they might be challenging. I looked through more papers that had to be signed. Medical releases, codes of conduct, textbook agreements, lunchtime passes. Lunch. I thought about the only peaceful part of my day. The part of the day that filled me with anticipation for to-morrow. My eyes glazed over as I stared at the pile, and I felt my pillow reach up and grab my head . . .

Green. Green. The cool green grass on my cheek. Bits of golden sun break through the giant leafy canopy, and then blue . . . not the soft blue sky, but icy, breath-catching blue, wash-ing over me, making my skin tingle . . . clear, penetrating blue that reminds me that I am seventeen years old, that I still want to laugh, dream, hope . . . love. The blackness that hugs my soul retreats . . .

"KAIT! DINNER! Your turn to set the table!"

Abby's whining voice jolted me awake. It was nearly dark. I sprang up from my bed, grabbed the pile of pa-pers, and joined my mom and sister in the kitchen. I set the table, laying my handful of papers down where my dad would have sat.

We held hands while my mom said a quick prayer for our food, the crops, my dad, for everything—but the Crutchfields. We never prayed for them.

"So, tell me about your days," my mom said. "How did it go?"

Abby rattled on and on while I picked at my spaghetti. "... and then I saw Carrie Adams! I haven't seen her since first grade! And in my English class I sit right between *two* hunks!" Abby dropped her jaw and fanned herself. "They are gorgeous! I couldn't listen to a word the teacher said!"

"Maybe you should ask the teacher if you can move," my mom suggested.

"Yeah, right," Abby went on. "I could probably sell my seat to the highest bidder! And then at lunch the girls from soccer introduced me to everyone. I'll never remember all their names! There was this one—"

"What about you, Kaitlin?" my mom interrupted. "Did you meet anyone?"

My mom and Abby stared at me with expectant eyes. I knew what they wanted to hear. A lie was justified.

I swallowed my mouthful of spaghetti. "Yes. I met someone. A boy."

"Does he have a name?" my mom asked.

I rolled his name around on my tongue before I whispered it. "Bram."

I expected Abby to make fun of the unusual name, but she just gave me an odd glance and looked back down at her plateful of spaghetti, without another word. It wasn't like Abby at all.

It was quiet for a long while, except for the clinking of our forks against our plates, the distant barking of Moe outside, and the gurgling sound of Abby pouring more milk. My mother stopped eating and shifted in her seat.

"I have some news, too," she said.

Abby and I put down our forks. Her voice made my stomach jump, and I could feel my throat tighten. My mother never "had news." I looked at her eyes.

I didn't want news.

"It's your father," she said. "He's coming home."

Chapter 4

THE SECOND DAY OF SCHOOL was worse than the first. Every step I took burned all the way up to my brain. My dad was coming home, and I was on the very land he loathed. In the camp of the enemy. I loved my dad. I felt like a traitor. It was still five weeks before he would be paroled—he had earned work credits to shorten his two-year prison term for manslaughter. That would give my mom time to break the news to him . . . to tell him where Abby and I went to school. It was all I could think about as I tried to take notes in each class. I bolted from my seat when the fourth-period bell rang.

"Hey, Kaitlin! What's your hurry?"

The Bookends were right behind me. I ignored them and walked faster, praying they wouldn't follow me. My prayers were answered. Their attention was redirected as soon as we passed the snack window. Thank God. I was looking forward to lunch and being alone . . . well, almost alone.

I arrived at the courtyard; Bram, a few minutes later. He nodded and smiled at me before he lay down on his grassy knoll and closed his eyes. It was only a nod . . . only a smile, but my fingers trembled as I wrote in my journal. A short while later I watched as he sat up and pulled his sketch pad from his backpack. We each sat there in our own worlds, releasing our hearts onto paper, and I wondered if the images he laid down brought order to his life . . . the way my words did for me. He caught me in another stare, but this time I was not mortified. I felt the persistent blush move across my cheeks, but it only felt warm. His piercing blue eyes seemed somehow . . . familiar, and that vague familiarity, again, made me catch my breath. When the bell rang, he stuffed his pad in his backpack and awkwardly raised his hand to me.

"Bye," he said.

I floated to my next class.

IT WAS CRAZY. I was supposed to be hating school—and I was. Really. But lunch wasn't exactly school. Was it? I didn't understand what was coming over me. I couldn't get him out of my thoughts. Was it because he spilled his feelings onto paper, too? Or was it something else . . . I didn't know. I only knew I felt angry at myself as I hurried to get ready for school the next day, irritated with myself as I glanced at my pocket mirror when the fourth-period bell rang, and then guilty as I rushed to lunch.

The guilt disappeared as soon as he made his entrance into the courtyard. It was like we had a quiet understanding. We didn't intrude on each other's space, but there was never a second we weren't aware of the other's presence. He pulled out his pad; I, my journal.

September 8
I swim in a swirling crystal ocean. Water as far as the eye can see, and my arms and legs grow weary. Then, in the midst of it all, an island rises from the blue and I stretch out on its warm sands. The heat caresses my cheek, the sand molds to my body, hugging me. I never want to leave . . . I am safe.

"Poetry?"

I was jerked from the island back to the courtyard. He—*he*—was talking to me.

"Huh?" *Brilliant, Kaitlin.* Master of words. Huh.

"Are you writing poetry?" he asked again.

"No, uh, no." *Composure, Kaitlin. Composure. Think.* "Just thoughts, glimpses, things running through my head." I willed my face not to turn red.

He smiled and nodded. An understanding.

The lunch bell rang.

"See you tomorrow," he said.

"Sure. Tomorrow," I answered. I watched him walk away. *Tomorrow.*

I don't remember walking to my next class. I didn't see the walkway, the door, my seat. I couldn't hear the teacher talk when she began her lecture. I saw clumps of blond hair, a wisp falling over one eyebrow. I saw brown arms against a white T-shirt. I saw a tentative smile, a busy hand sketching. I heard a low voice and felt the texture of warm sand caressing my cheek. I was immersed in blue eyes washing over me, refreshing my soul. I heard the words, over and over, creating their own symphony . . . *See you tomorrow.*

By the time I got home, I decided I was a lunatic. Certified. Or maybe I was just pathetically needy. Or better yet, maybe I could just chalk it up to hormones. But it didn't feel like hormones. It felt like more. A bond maybe. There had been boys at Holy Trinity, but never one who haunted my thoughts. Never one who sent a wild rush pulsing through my veins just by the mere memory of his eyes. Was this what it felt like to be seventeen? Was *this* the normal I craved? Self-absorbed? Indulgent? Entertaining fantasies I dared not whisper?

I was brought back to reality when my mom got home. The slamming door jolted my daydreams.

"What's wrong?" I asked. I jumped up from our fraying blue couch.

My mom closed her eyes and put her fingers to her temples. "Just a sec. Let me think."

I could tell she was trying to calm down. She was tired of crying, too. But her lip started to tremble anyway. "I forgot to place the order for our winter seed—I thought

Rick was going to do it—but he said that I told him—oh! It doesn't matter! The bottom line is the seed will be late."

I pulled my mom over to the couch and sat her down. Her hands shook in mine. I squeezed them to try to stop her trembling. She poured out all her fears. "Our winter crop is so important, Kaitlin. The lawyers have been hounding me for more money, and when I tell them I don't have it, they tell me to sell some land. I tell them we are not like those damn Crutchfields! They don't understand. And the taxes are overdue. The winter crop will keep our heads above water, so I can't mess up. I've got to—"

I pulled her close to me. "It's okay, Mom. It will all work out." I held her tight, and she sobbed on my shoulder. There were always more tears.

"It's just that with your father coming home—I just want it all to be here—ready for him—like it was before. Before *they* turned our lives upside down. There's so much to get ready. It's just so hard . . ."

We held each other. There was nothing left to say. I knew she wasn't crying just over the seed, or the lawyers, or the taxes. Those worries had always been there. It was fear. The lost months. Wondering if things could ever return to how they were before. I was afraid, too. I hadn't seen my dad since he was carted off to prison. He refused to allow us to visit. The Malone daughters, he said, would never step foot in a prison. They would never see their dad in a prison uniform. Did the Crutchfields know about that? Did they care? Did empty shells ever care? It was their lies that put him there. Someday they would know. Someday.

"I'm sorry, Kaitlin. I don't mean to put all this on you." My mom wiped her eyes and stood up. The wave of fear had passed.

I tucked a stray curl behind her ear. "It's okay, Mom. We just have to stick together. Right?"

"Right." She brushed her hand along my cheek and smiled. "Now come tell me about your day while I fix dinner."

I told her the details about my classes but only briefly mentioned lunch. I still felt guilty that there was something I liked about Twin Oaks High School. Something that made me look forward to the next day.

"Well, I'm glad you've met at least one person. An artist yet!" she said as she swished a head of lettuce under the faucet. "What did you say his name was?"

"Bram." Bram. Just a boy from a school I hated. A boy I had only exchanged a dozen words with. I should be able to erase him from my thoughts.

I should.

On Thursday I waited for the Bookends to leave the classroom first. I was catching on to their game, and I decided I would play it better. It was only seconds before their stomachs overruled their brains, and they were drawn away to the lunch lines. I hurried to the courtyard. The sun sizzled and I felt damp wisps of hair sticking to my forehead. My peach tank top clung to my back. I looked forward to my cool, shady spot on the planter.

When I arrived, Bram was already there—in my spot. I hesitated. I wasn't sure where I should sit. Next to him? In his spot under the tree? He raised his eyes to mine. My question was answered. I sat down on the brick planter a few feet from him.

"Hi. I hope you don't mind me taking over your spot. I'm Bram."

"Yes. I know. I mean, I heard your friends call your name the other day. I'm Kait." I held my hand out, and then wished I hadn't. It was so formal, but he took it anyway and held it longer than he needed to. There was a bond. I was right.

"I just wanted to show something to you." He pulled his sketch pad from his backpack and flipped back a few pages. He turned the pad for me to see.

My mouth fell open. It was me. A few spare lines, the beginning of a face trying to emerge from a sea of white. But me. Definitely me. When? How? But then I knew— the glances were not at the buildings or trees. They were at me.

"Of course, it's not finished," he went on. "Just an initial sketch, but I wanted to make sure it was okay with you, that is, if I can keep looking at you—I mean, sketch you, over the next few days. Are you okay with that? I need the practice. Will you be here?" He drew in a deep breath.

"Yes, I'll be here and, yes, I'm okay with that." My heart was already melting at the way he stumbled over his words. Was his artwork that important to him . . . or was it possible that I made him nervous? I looked back at the sketch.

"Just these few simple lines are beautiful. I don't know what to say."

"Don't say anything. I'm just glad I have such a good model."

My chest did a flip-flop.

"You're new here, aren't you?" he asked.

"Yes. It's my first year. How did you know?"

"You're different."

God! Was I that out of step?

He must have sensed my embarrassment or my cheeks were tattling on me because he quickly explained further.

"No, I mean a *good* kind of different. You don't mind being alone. You don't chatter on and on like some people I know."

I smiled. I didn't know what to say—as usual. I looked back to his drawing. "This is really good. It looks so professional."

"Thanks, but I still have a lot to learn."

"Oh, are you going to study art in college?"

The smile faded from his face. I knew I had asked the wrong question.

"I was going to," he said. "I had planned on going to the Design Institute in L.A.—but I don't think it's going to work out." He hesitated for a moment and added, "I've had some family problems. You know how that goes."

I nodded. Yes. I knew.

It *was* more than hormones. There was a bond. I knew it. I wanted to know him better—I wanted to know everything about him, and I wanted him to know me. He must have read my thoughts.

His smile returned. "I'm glad you like the sketch. Maybe someday I can read some of the things you write." Instead of being frightened by the idea, I felt warmed by it. I looked straight into his eyes, unembarrassed. One, two, three seconds, the gaze continued.

I smiled. "Yes, and someday I'd like to share them with you."

Chapter 5

EACH DAY our brief talks were hesitant, shy, but for me, filled with expectation. By the middle of the following week, I could barely hide my eagerness to go to school. I was convinced Bram had to be a gift from God, a gift, like manna, to help me survive the Crutchfield wilderness.

On Wednesday as I got ready for school, Abby walked into my room unannounced. She observed me in my bra and underwear holding up a red top in front of my dresser mirror. Two other tops lay on the floor at my feet. She let out an exasperated sigh and rolled her eyes.

"Get out!" I yelled. Standard protocol between us.

Abby didn't listen. No surprise. She planted herself against the doorjamb. "Since when did you start caring about your clothes? Besides, what difference does it make what you wear? No one ever sees you anyway."

"Oh, sure. In a school of almost three thousand students, no one sees me. Right."

"I never see you at lunch. Just where *do* you go?" The way she asked made me think she knew exactly where I went. She had always been on the sneaky side. The last thing I needed was her taunting me about Bram.

"None of your business—now get out! I've got to get ready or we'll be late!" I raised my voice to the proper decibel to assure her I was through with the conversation and the next step would be calling Mom. Standard protocol, too. She left, her brows knit together, not like she was angry, but more like she was puzzled. I hoped her little freshman brain wouldn't short out.

I threw the red top down and picked up a plain white T. No sense in giving her fuel.

In spite of my free-for-all with my clothes, we still managed to get to school on time. When the fourth-period bell finally rang, I was ready to hurry to the courtyard, but Mr. Bailey held me back. He complimented me on my "exceptional" performance on my first assignment, an essay on American isolationism. I thanked him and left. I was wasting precious minutes of my lunch. As soon as I walked out the door, the Bookends stepped in front of me, blocking my path.

"Beautiful *and* smart!"

"Yeah, you're quite the wonder!"

"What a babe!"

Why did they have to harass *me*? Was I an easy target? I tried to step around them, but they carefully maneuvered in front of me again. I felt the flush that was my trademark spreading across my face. It was further humiliation. "C'mon, Kaitlin, we're just trying to be friendly. Don't you want to be friendly?"

Friendly like vipers. But I couldn't force the words from my mouth. I pushed my way through them, triggering their laughter. They had their fun for the day. They didn't follow me and went off to feed their perverted lumps of flesh.

I focused on my path to the courtyard, trying to erase the image of a slimy piece of food wedged in Bookend #2's grinning front teeth. Even with the ninety-plus-degree heat, I shivered. *A gift. Yes, Bram is a gift to help me survive this Crutchfield nightmare.* He was the only bright spot in my day. He made me feel that some small, miserable piece of my seventeen-year-old life was normal—or could be.

"Hi." Bram smoothed a stray lock back with one hand and smiled.

The tension melted from my shoulders. I could almost forget that I was at school at all. I sat down on the brick planter, measuring my distance as I sat. Not too close to imply that I thought there was something going on between us, but not so far as to imply that I didn't want there to be. "Hi," I said. Hi. My muscles were made of vanilla pudding. There was no tension, anywhere—at least not the bad kind. I pulled a fat green apple from my backpack, twisting the stem with my fingers.

He nodded toward his backpack. "I'm almost done."

"With my portrait? Can I see?"

"Tomorrow. I'll show you tomorrow—if that's okay. I just want to put some finishing touches on it—and to think about it a little more."

"Think about it? You *think* about your drawing?" I edged closer to him, hoping I didn't sound totally ignorant about art. "I mean, I just thought with drawing it was more of a seeing thing."

"You can't see everything with your eyes. I learned that in Drawing 101. Like my teacher said, there is a roundness, a depth, a hidden side to everything that holds it together...like this—" He grabbed my hand that was clutching the apple and cupped it in his. My hand burned with a thousand tiny explosions, but I didn't pull away. He guided my fingers around the apple as he explained. "When you've held an apple in your hand, felt its smooth skin, felt its weight, ran your fingers around it, maybe taken a bite out of it and tasted it, you know there is more to it than a round green circle; you understand its hidden side and its depth. When you understand what holds something together, your drawing will show that." He lifted his eyes from the apple to my face. "But some things are more complicated than apples; you can't hold them or dissect them—so you have to think about them..." He squeezed my hand tighter around the apple. "You think about them, sometimes in the dark...when you're alone...You think about the hidden parts and what holds them together." He let go of my hand.

The apple rolled from my vanilla pudding fingers to the ground. I finally took a breath.

Bram jumped up to retrieve my dented apple. "Sorry." He rubbed it on his shirt to get the grit off. "I think you can still eat it."

No matter how dented, nothing in the world could stop me from eating that apple now.

THE NEXT DAY I very nearly ran to the courtyard. I moved so fast out of fourth period, I caught the Bookends by surprise and they were left in my dust. The night before I had hardly slept, tossing and turning. With the September heat pressing down on me, I skimmed my bare legs across the sheets searching for coolness in the blackness. Searching for coolness, rest, peace. Unlike Bram, my thinking didn't bring me insight but restlessness, searching for answers in the void of my room. I wondered, over and over and over again, was it merely an art lesson that had passed between us or something more? It had to be more. I needed it to be more.

And who had I become? A few weeks ago I was repulsed at the thought of attending a Crutchfield school. Now each day I was filled with anticipation. It didn't seem right. What would my father think? But I wasn't embracing the Crutchfields, only finding refuge in one small corner of this ugly nightmare they had created. I was a Malone. I was surviving.

I slowed as I neared the courtyard, conscious of the dampness on my neck, hoping I didn't look like a sweaty mess. He might reconsider his drawing. Today he was lying in the shade on the grassy knoll, his eyes staring up into the leafy canopy above him, studying it. I suppose he looked at everything a little differently than most people. I liked that.

I noisily scuffed my shoes on the sidewalk as I approached. He glanced over and, seeing me, he jumped up, scooping his backpack along with him. I sat down on a section of the brick planter where a large ficus tree offered some shade. He joined me, sitting close enough to take advantage of the shade, too. I wished the tree were smaller.

"It's done. Want to see it?"

I nodded, unable to trust myself, afraid of blurting out like a frog, an off-key, too eager "Yes!" The anticipation, as he pulled his sketchbook out, unleashed a fluttering wave through my body. He turned back a few pages and gently pulled out a sheet and handed it to me.

I held the paper in my hands. It wasn't what I expected. The simple elegant lines had been transformed into an intricate, luxurious weave of strokes, crossing at perfect angles to reveal planes, strands, crevices, and shadows. The sheer beauty of the lines alone mesmerized me. But then they gathered together in perfect form, like words gather together in a flawless poem, to create the image that was me. *Me.* Not just the shape of my face or the length of my hair, but the hidden parts. The frightened me, the dreamy me . . . the yearning me. It swirled around on the page with my eyes, my hair, my half-parted lips. I couldn't speak. What else had he seen? I brushed at the flush rising on my cheeks, hoping he wouldn't notice.

"It's a gift," I finally whispered. "You truly have a gift. It's amazing."

"You like it, then?"

I nodded. No words could convey the emotion surging through me. The bond had just deepened. And somehow I think he understood that. My nod was enough. He smiled and that seemed like the seal on our wordless exchange.

A warm breeze caught the paper in my hands and almost whisked it away. He scooted closer and we looked together at the drawing again. My eyes followed the sensitive lines, from my forehead, to floating wisps of hair, down to my neckline. His initials were lightly signed at the base of the neck—like a kiss. My skin tingled. I wondered if his did, too. My fingers gently touched the small letters.

"B. C.?" I asked.

He smiled. "Yeah. Bram—Bram Crutchfield."

Chapter 6

THE PAPER SLIPPED from my fingers. The courtyard vibrated around me. Bram jumped up to retrieve the paper from the ground, and I noticed he seemed to move in slow motion. The entire world was screeching to a halt in short jerky movements as my mind raced past it. Order. I needed order—but there was none. Bram turned with the paper in hand and lifted his piercing blue eyes to mine. He was speaking, but his words weren't reaching my ears. His eyes. His familiar blue eyes. I *had* seen them before—a hundred times on the evening news—the piercing blue eyes of the dead Robert Crutchfield.

"Kait? Kait? Are you okay?"

Bram slipped the portrait back into my hands. Bram *Crutchfield.*

I felt a wave of nausea.

"I have to go. I have to go." I'm not sure how many times I repeated the same sentence. I picked up my backpack and ran from the courtyard. I could hear Bram calling after me, but the words were a jumble. I ran all the way to my car. If students stared at me, I didn't know. It was like I was running down a long dark tunnel that was closing in on me and my car was my only escape. When I reached it, my dizzy head won, and I leaned over and threw up. Again, I didn't know if anyone saw. I didn't care. I climbed into the front seat and leaned back. I fumbled for my water bottle and pushed the wet strands of hair from my forehead. I took a sip and then poured the rest over my face, trying to wash away the last five minutes. I closed my eyes, trying to block out Bram's face.

Crutchfield. Crutchfield. It was a horrible drumbeat, pounding in my head.

My eyes shot open. Abby! That strange look on her face at dinner that night. She knew! Of course, she knew! But *how much* did she know? Did she know I had not gone to bed a single night since I saw him without his name lingering on my lips? Did she know the warm rush I felt every time I remembered his blue eyes looking into mine? Could she possibly know my secret, shameful dreams of . . . *the enemy?*

I shoved my key into the ignition. How could I have been so stupid? So deceived? I hated the Crutchfields. I hated Bram. I would never go back to the courtyard. Never.

It wasn't until I pulled onto our dirt road that I realized I had ditched my last class. If my mom was at the Malone Company offices, she would see the telltale trail of dust from my car and wonder why I was home so early. I couldn't tell her the truth. I had to have a story ready.

I was sick. That was it. And it was true, really. I ran up to my room and shoved the portrait under my bed. I wondered why I didn't just rip it into a thousand pieces and flush it down the toilet. *Just do it, Kaitlin! Do it!*

I snatched it back from under my bed and ran down the hallway to the bathroom. I stood there over the toilet, my tears falling into the bowl, my hands shaking as I held the paper.

Rip it up! Flush it! Now! But...I couldn't. What was happening? I hated the Crutchfields. Because of them, my father was in prison. They had torn my family apart. They had always made the Malones' lives difficult. The sins go back generations. From squabbles over property lines, deliberate brushfires, grievances filed with the city, even fistfights. They had proven over and over that they were scum. My grandmother had passed the warnings on to my father, my father to me. I hated them. I did. They deserved to be hated.

The paper trembled in my hands. *Do it, Kaitlin. Do it!* But instead, I clutched the picture to my chest and fell to my knees, sobbing.

I didn't deserve to call myself a Malone.

Chapter 7

"YOU THREW UP right in the parking lot? God! Don't park in that spot today!"

Abby was being her usual sympathetic self. "Are you sure no one saw you? How embarrassing!"

I turned our old Buick into the now infamous parking lot. "Don't worry, Abby. Your reputation is still intact. No one knows who I am anyway."

Abby was quiet for a few seconds, then asked, "What about *Bram*?"

The knot in my stomach turned. I knew she was fishing.

"I don't even know a Bram. I just heard his name tossed around by a group of girls, so I mentioned it to Mom. I know she wants me to meet people."

"Oh."

She didn't believe me. I could tell by her silence. But for now it was the best explanation I could give. As immature as Abby was, I still didn't want her to think I was a traitor. Some things mattered. On some things, the Malones had to stick together. I was never going to see Bram again, so it was almost the truth.

As usual, Abby bounded out of the car as soon as it stopped, and I was left alone. Twin Oaks High School looked different today. More frightening.

"Bye, Abby," I whispered. But she didn't hear me. She was gone.

It was more frightening, because with everything I now knew, I *still* wanted to be here. A monster lurked in my soul, digging, picking, and every time I tried to hide a thought, it pushed it to the surface. I hated the fleeting glimpses that kept intruding. Blue. Clumps of golden hair. A warm hand holding mine. A white T-shirt. Paper with perfect smudges. A hesitant smile . . . *Stop it, Kaitlin!*

I needed order. I would write in my journal during class. I'd pour out my fragmented thoughts and be done with it. I'd forget Bram Crutchfield, the courtyard, the whole week. I'd forget that I wanted to be here.

By the end of fourth period, there were exactly two words in my journal.

September 17

I looked up at the clock. Five minutes left. I still had to figure out where I was going to eat lunch today. The courtyard seemed to be the only empty place on the crowded campus, but it was out of the question. My hot, steamy car was not an alternative. Damn! Why should I have to run and hide? I found the courtyard first! Why should a Malone let a Crutchfield win again? I should stand my ground. Let *him* find a new place to eat! When the bell rang and the Bookends followed me out the door, I had resolved what to do.

"Hey, Kaitlin. It's Friday. Party time!"

"Yeah. Whooh. C'mon, Kaitlin!"

I whipped around. It was not a good day to harass me. I walked up to within inches of Bookend #1's face. "Get—a—life!" I reached over and flipped Bookend #2's hat from his head. "Party on." I turned back around and stomped off. I was prepared to take back the courtyard— it was mine.

My footsteps kept time with my beating heart as I walked. What did he mean, *family problems*? What kind of problems could the Crutchfields have? I'd tell him about problems! I'd finally let him—let everyone know—just what I thought of him. Someday! My "someday" had come! My last steps into the courtyard were practically a run. He was there, waiting on the planter. I stumbled to a stop.

He lifted his eyes to mine. A smile followed. The anger that had arrogantly pushed me into the courtyard was retreating. The familiar warm rush that haunted me every time I looked at him spread through my stomach, my chest, all the way out to my fingertips. It paralyzed me like a powerful drug. Time moved in slow motion again. I hated the Crutchfields, but . . . did I really hate

Bram? He was just a boy. What did he know about lies and hatred? Maybe nothing. Just because he was a Crutchfield didn't mean he was *like* the Crutchfields. Maybe he was different. One of them could be different. Maybe.

"Hi." He stood up and walked over to meet me. "You okay? You left so fast yesterday, I thought maybe my picture made you sick."

Now was my chance. I had a Crutchfield in my clutches and I could let him have it, but the drug that paralyzed me also numbed my anger. I was the lunatic once again. "No! I loved your picture. I just—forgot to turn something in—in my last class, that is." My mind moved at warp speed trying to sound believable. "I didn't want it to be marked late." I couldn't believe the words were coming from my mouth. *Stop lying, Kait. Tell him the truth. Tell him who you are.*

"That's a relief. I thought maybe I had blown it." He grabbed my arm and led me over to the planter. We sat down. "I don't mean to come on strong or anything. I just..." I watched him struggle for his words. He was vulnerable. Like me. I wanted to reach out, help him, tell him I understood everything. It wasn't his fault he was born into a miserable family. "I just think that you are someone I could be good friends with."

Friends. My guilt surged. Friends don't lie. "I want to be your friend, too, Bram." *Tell him, Kait. Tell him, now.* But I was the daughter of a Crutchfield killer. My insides twisted. I had to tell him. My nails dug into my palms. He was different. He would understand.

"Bram! What's goin' on?" A strolling group approached. Three boys. Two girls.

Bram stood and punched one in the arm. "Hey, Matt! Nothin's going on—except that it's Friday!"

"Yeah. A bunch of us are going to Red's tonight for pizza and then hang out somewhere. Wanna go?"

"Sounds cool." Bram turned to me. "Can you go?"

No. Of course I couldn't go. I couldn't hang out with a Crutchfield. It was ridiculous. "Sure. Sounds like fun," I said. What was happening? It was like the drug had taken over my thoughts, actions...the drug I craved, called Bram.

The group all had their attention on me. They surely wondered who this person was that their "king" was hanging out with. I slid my hands into my jeans. I wasn't going to be a nerd again and hold out my hand. "Hi. I'm Kait M—"

I froze and then swallowed hard.

"Hampton. Kait Hampton. It's good to meet you."

I had to lie, I told myself. It was too soon. I didn't know him well enough yet to know how he would react. I had been filled with a fierce tornado of emotions when he told me. A tornado that made me throw up in the parking lot. I didn't want that for him. And I couldn't tell him in front of his friends. I would tell him later. It was only a temporary lie.

Chapter 8

"CAN SOMEONE GET THAT!"

The phone rang and rang, and I was already running late. I had promised Bram I would meet him at 5:30 at Red's. He wanted to pick me up, and I told another lie about how I was going to be out already and it would be easier just to meet him there. Everyone, especially the Crutchfields, knew who lived on this piece of land. There was no way he could pick me up.

Abby walked into the room with her headphones on. Jeez! I grabbed the phone from the receiver. "Hello!" I yelled.

"Collect call from Garner Malone. Will you accept the charges?"

"Yes," I whispered. It felt like every ounce of my blood was pooling in my feet.

There was a long moment of silence and then, "Abby?"

"No, Dad. It's Kait."

"Kait. How are you, baby?"

"Good. How about you?"

The words all seemed so functional. Saying the right thing at the right time. I felt like such a fake. I was getting ready to go out with one of the people that had put the man on the phone behind bars. It didn't matter that I hadn't killed Robert Crutchfield, or that Bram had probably never set eyes on my father. The Crutchfields and Malones had an understanding of hate—the same way dogs detest cats. I was talking with one of my own, while I collaborated with one of *them*. I was worse than them all.

We continued to chat about superficial things like he was away on a business trip instead of in prison. "I love you, too, Dad. I'll get Mom." I wondered as I went to get my mom if my voice sounded different to him, the way his did to me. Did I sound like I was hiding something? Could he hear the lies beating at my conscience the way he could when I was small? Was I convincing when I said I was just going out with some friends? Nobody particular? And why did he sound different to me? Why did he sound... like a stranger? Or at least different than he had a week ago when I talked to him? Why did it feel so different now?

When my mom picked up the phone, I felt relieved. It gave me some distance, at least for the moment, from my lies. My thoughts turned back to the evening ahead of me. It was 5:25. I was going to be late. I grabbed my keys and drove as fast as I could to Red's.

It was amazing how easily I became Kait Hampton. And as I sat next to Bram, eating pizza, laughing with his friends, feeling special because Bram saved the spot next to him for me, I was glad I had lied.

Matt sat across from us, shoving straws up his nose, apparently trying to impress Jenny, who was sitting next to him. It didn't work, because she turned her attention to me and asked, "So where did you say you went to school last year?"

"Holy Trinity Academy."

"Oh, is your family really religious?"

"No. Not really."

"Then why did you go there?"

Jenny seemed friendly enough, but I didn't know if she was just trying to make small talk or if she was digging for something deeper. The pizza parlor suddenly seemed warmer.

"I—uh—my parents liked the small size, I guess." *Good, Kaitlin. Sound casual.* I wiped the corners of my mouth, trying to make my jaw relax.

"So why did you switch?"

Why did she ask so many questions? Especially since I was running out of answers. Jenny was starting to get on my nerves. My fingers returned to the corners of my mouth.

"Because she heard that I went to Twin Oaks." Bram saved me. He looked at me with those eyes that turned my bones to jelly. I forgot about Jenny. "Right?" he asked.

"Oh, sure," I teased, but in my heart I was saying "right" a thousand times over, "right."

"Hey! Look who finally made it!" Matt said.

We all turned and looked to see Jason walking toward our table. My heart exploded in my chest when I saw who walked with him. Oh my God! It couldn't be! She saw me at the same time, and her eyes grew wide with surprise. *Oh my God! Oh my God! Think, Kaitlin!*

I jumped up and threw open my arms. "Becky!" I hugged her, and whispered in her ear. "Don't say anything! Please! They don't know who I am." My knees felt weak as I pulled away and looked into Becky's face. She never missed a beat.

"Hey, *girl*! I haven't seen you forever!"

"How do you two know each other?" Jason asked.

"We both went to Holy Trinity," I answered. "Becky, I was just going to the rest room. Come with me, okay?" I grabbed her hand and dragged her along, knowing the whole group had their eyes on us. Becky didn't resist. She knew Kaitlin Malone didn't act like a lunatic without good reason. We burst into the bathroom.

"What's the big secret, Kait?" she asked the minute the door closed behind us. "Why are you acting so—"

"That's Bram *Crutchfield* out there."

Becky's voice went up three decibels. "What! Are you craz—"

I slapped my hand over her mouth. "*Shhh!* It gets

worse! I'm crazy about him, Becky!" I lowered my hand from her mouth when I was certain she wouldn't scream.

"Oh my God, Kaitlin," she said slowly. "And he doesn't know who you are?"

I shook my head. "None of them do. My mom made us enroll as Hamptons." I wondered if she could take more. "And I have a favor to ask. Bram wanted to pick me up tonight and I made up an excuse. If he asks again, can I use your address?"

"What?" Becky yelled.

My hand went back over her mouth. "Please, Becky. I don't have a choice. I can't tell him where I live. *Please*. It's just temporary."

Becky closed her eyes and shook her head. "I can't believe this, Kait. It's so—not you. Does your family know about him?"

"Are you kidding? No way!"

"What about Abby? That little squirrel figures things out pretty fast. Hasn't she seen you with him at school?"

"No. I don't think so. But I think she's suspicious. Anyway, about the address, can I use yours for a while—just in case he should ask?"

Becky rolled her eyes and let out a long sigh. "Oh, what a tangled web we weave . . . I suppose for now . . . *mi casa es su casa*."

"Thanks, Beck."

Becky reached for the door, then stopped. "So you have the hots for a Crutchfield," she said, shaking her head. "I never would have guessed *that* in a million years."

"It's not 'the hots,' Becky. It's different."

"Yeah, sure. You've known him—what? Two weeks? And you're already madly in love?" She shook her head again. "C'mon, we'd better go back before they think we're constipated or something." She swung her arm around my shoulder and led me back out.

We slid back into the booth and introductions were finished. Becky then proceeded to chat away like I hadn't just revealed the secret of the century to her in the bathroom. She was amazing. Bram leaned over and whispered in my ear. I savored his warm breath on my skin.

"Your friend is nothing like you. She talks—a lot."

I smiled. That was Becky. Maybe that is why we hooked up. She was a good talker; I was a good listener. But she could be a good listener, too—when I needed it.

My skin continued to tingle where Bram's breath had touched it. Was Becky right? Was it only hormones?

"Sorry to break this up," Bram said when Becky took a breather, "but I gotta go. I promised my little brother I would bring him home some ice cream. He had a bad day at school."

"Hey! We just got here," Jason said.

"*You* just got here—we've been here for two hours. Besides, I'll see you tomorrow. Bring Becky."

Jason's eyes lit up. He obviously had "the hots" for Becky. "Yeah, right. Well, say hi to Josh for me."

I slid out of the booth to let Bram out, disappointed that the evening was ending so early. I would have to wait until Monday to see him again.

"Kait, you want to walk me out?" Bram asked.

I stood there like a dope. I was afraid to walk him out. I wasn't experienced with boys, the way Becky was. I wasn't sure what "walking him out" meant, but my fear wasn't as strong as my desire to be with him. "Sure," I said.

We walked out to the parking lot. Perhaps now would be a good time to tell him who I was. My heart pounded faster at the thought. Bram had one of those shiny white Jeeps I had despised on the first day of school, and he unlocked it with a remote attached to his key ring. It reminded me that he was indeed a Crutchfield.

I tried to erase the thought from my mind by remembering he was doing something sweet for his little brother. "So why did your brother have a bad day at school?" I assumed it was something trivial, like Abby often complained about—she forgot her homework, or the teacher called on her and she didn't know the answer.

Bram leaned against his open car door. He hesitated, like he wasn't certain he wanted to tell me. "Josh is in kindergarten. Today they were supposed to draw pictures of their families. He drew all of us—except my dad. You see, my dad is dead."

My heart raced faster, and I looked down at my feet. I felt like I was hearing something that wasn't really meant for my ears—like I was eavesdropping—but Bram went on. "When a couple of the kids told him he had to draw his dad, too, he drew my dad's gravestone, and then they all started laughing." Bram's voice cracked and I looked up. His jaw was tight, and I saw a vein bulge near his temple that I hadn't noticed before. I wanted to change the subject. I knew what made that vein pulse. I recognized it as surely as I did the furrow across my grandmother's brow . . . my own brow. Rage. Hate. I wanted to change the subject back to pizza, Becky, anything, because every word brought me back to who I was.

But he went on.

"It's a terrible thing to lose your dad—especially the way we did." *Stop, Bram! Please, stop!* "But it's even worse when you are just a little kid. Josh still doesn't quite understand it all. I guess I don't either, really."

I felt a horrible pounding in my head. I didn't want to hear about the Crutchfields' pain. It was mine. The pain had always been mine, not theirs. I felt like something I had always clutched close to my heart was being ripped away. Stolen.

My horror must have shown on my face. When Bram looked up into my eyes, he seemed startled. "I'm sorry. I didn't mean to get so heavy. The reason I asked you to walk out with me is I wanted to tell you about a barbecue we're having at my house tomorrow. No big thing, a few kids from school, and we might go swimming. Can you come?"

Eating pizza with the enemy was one thing, but going to their house was another. How could I possibly go to his home and maybe even meet other Crutchfields? It was too bizarre to consider. Bram was different, but the Crutchfields were still the Crutchfields. I held on to my pain, the foundation of the Malone hate, my legacy.

"I don't think so, Bram. I have to work tomorrow, and then I have a lot of homework I need—"

"Wait a sec!" He leaned in his Jeep and brought out a pencil and a scrap piece of paper. "What's your phone number? I'll call you just in case you change your mind."

No way could a Crutchfield be calling my house. "Why don't you let me call you? We have a block on our phone because of some wacko calls we were getting." Gosh, I was getting good at this.

He quickly scrawled his number on the paper and handed it to me. "We're not getting together until around four. Maybe you can work it out somehow."

The pulsing vein was gone, and he looked into my eyes without blinking. I was immersed in an ocean of blue, drowning, and I didn't care.

"I'll try," I said, as I took the paper from his hand. But I already knew that, somehow, I would work it out. I liked Bram. More than liked him. I didn't want to. I wanted to hate him. The way I had always hated the Crutchfields. Secretly I wanted to find a flaw, the vein of ugliness that ran through all of the other Crutchfields. The ugliness I had always been told was there. But if it had somehow skipped Bram, it was surely in the others. It had to be. I was afraid of losing the Malone hate, because if I didn't have that, I had really lost everything. If there was no "them" . . . could there really be an "us"?

"I'll try to make it," I said.

I had to know about the others.

Chapter 9

September 18
The ledge grew narrow. I scooted closer to the cold wall
behind me. My feet were firmly planted on the hard con-
crete beneath me . . . but still, I could feel the hard sur-
face change to warm sand. My toes relished the rich
texture, even as I felt the ledge that held me fall away.
How much closer to the wall could I hug? Or should I
just fall away with the sand, giving in to its warm
temptation?

"WHEN WERE THESE PICKED?"

A woman with dimpled cheeks and a big straw hat
was holding up a tomato. I closed my journal and remembered I was supposed to be working.

"Just this morning," I told her, feeling pride as a wide grin spread across her face. The Malones may not have much, but what we did have counted.

"Can you bag me up a dozen and two of those cucumbers, too?"

"Yes, ma'am." Our roadside vegetable stand gave Abby and me spending money and helped with some of the household bills, too. I traded shifts with Abby, so I could have the afternoon free. I knew she would happily agree. Both of us hated getting up early on Saturday mornings, so she was a little surprised when I offered to take her turn at the morning shift.

"The ones you buy at the supermarket just never have much taste. Closer to cardboard," she said, as she opened her wallet.

"Not even close to these," I agreed. All those fancy markets that dotted the Crutchfield landscape couldn't compete with the Malone vegetables. "Stop by again soon," I said, handing her the change. We did a fair business, and in the spring when we sold strawberries, we often had long lines on the weekends. I wiped the sweat from my forehead as the woman maneuvered her huge Cadillac out of our small dirt parking lot. It was blistering hot, and I was a drippy, dusty mess, but Abby would be here in fifteen more minutes. Plenty of time to go home and get cleaned up before I went to Bram's. My stomach jumped. I couldn't believe I was actually going to do it. It almost felt illegal—or worse. I couldn't even count how many lies had brought me to this point. Last night I had lied again to Mom and Abby.

"Yeah, Becky is having a few friends over, and then we might go to the beach or something." I used my most casual voice, defying even Abby to become suspicious. The lies were becoming easier. But again, I reminded myself, it was only temporary—just until I felt it was safe to tell. They couldn't handle the truth right now. It was still hard for me to accept. Only a week ago I had hated the faceless Crutchfields . . . but now one of them did have a face, and it wasn't the face I had imagined all the years of my childhood.

The back door of the stand opened and Abby walked in. She was ten minutes early. Not like Abby. I was wary.

"Hey, Kait. Hot enough for you?"

She was perky, too. My defenses shot up. "Yeah, Abby. It's hot. What's up? You're early."

"Eleven minutes. No big deal."

Wrong. Eleven minutes was a big deal to Abby, especially if it benefited me. She was usually ten minutes late. She started reorganizing the tomatoes into neat rows.

"So you're going to Becky's tonight, huh?"

"That's right."

"It's funny, but I started thinking about that last night in bed."

I knew there was something. I didn't say anything, waiting for her to drop the bomb.

"I remember a week ago at soccer practice, Becky's sister saying they were in the middle of a big remodel. Their house was a mess, and she and Becky were sleeping in the living room. I'm surprised Becky would have a few friends over, considering the mess and all."

It wasn't a statement. It was a trap, and Abby waited to catch me. Lying to Bram, his friends, my mom and dad had been surprisingly easy—but Abby was a problem. She hated the Crutchfields as much as any of us, and I knew she would not tolerate even the slightest degree of betrayal. I felt like she was always just one step behind me, tracking me, ready to close in for the kill. Abby was more experienced at this game, but I was learning fast.

"That's why I said we are going to the beach or something. Becky's is just the meeting place. You want to go?" My last words were sheer genius. I knew Abby already had plans for tonight, but inviting her to tag along was sure to confuse her.

She tweaked her head to the side and answered slowly, "No, uh, no thanks."

Inside, I was raising a triumphant fist into the air, but outside I maintained my casual indifference. "Whatever." I gathered my stuff together and started to leave.

"Thanks for the invite though. Say hi to Br—Becky for me."

Even in the scorching heat, a chill ran down my back. I hesitated as I opened the door. She was still nipping at my heels. "Sure," I said, and I let the door slam behind me.

When I got home, I forgot about Abby, tomatoes, and the Crutchfields. Thoughts of Bram were able to do that. I changed clothes three times, frustrated that I had become a caricature of Abby trying to find just the right outfit. I settled on a plain yellow tank and jean shorts. Would this be okay to wear to a *Crutchfield* house? My throat tightened and I prayed that my thoughts were confined to my head. My mother was in the next room, and if she knew, if she had even the slightest idea what I was about to do . . .

I picked up the phone and dialed Bram. I noticed the excitement in his voice when I told him I could make it after all.

"I'll come get you. Where do you live?" he asked.

"Oh, no. That's okay. Just give me directions."

His house was in an area of make-you-gag, filthy-rich homes. From the street all you can see are gates and long drives, and sometimes a glimpse through the landscape of a sprawling, magnificent house. I had always wondered who lived in that neighborhood. Now I knew. Would they even let my rusty Buick through their expensive gates? As I listened to the rich texture of Bram's voice, I even forgot about that. I just wanted to be there—with him.

"Kait, I can't describe it—you're the one who's good with words—but I just feel—I—" He hesitated. The short silence seemed an eternity. "I have been thinking about you a lot," he finally blurted out.

His words were good. Worth the awkward silence.

"I'm good at writing down words, Bram, but not very good at saying them. I—uh—" It was my turn to stumble. *Write it in your head, Kait, and then just say it.* But it wasn't that easy. I echoed his words. "I have been thinking a lot about you, too, Bram."

"I just feel like I can be myself with you . . . honest, I guess. I've never been like that with a girl before."

Honest. His words stabbed at my conscience.

What a fake I was. I would tell him. Tonight, when we were face-to-face. I had to tell him. There was something special . . . unusual . . . between us, and I couldn't risk losing it. He was not like the rest of the Crutchfields. He was different. He would understand.

"I feel the same, Bram," I whispered. "I'll be over soon." I said good-bye and gently replaced the receiver.

Once I gathered together my things, I couldn't move fast enough. If I hurried, maybe I wouldn't slip from the crumbling ledge I clung to. I could outrun my lies. It wasn't until I was on the quiet, twisting road searching for Bram's house that I slowed down. There were no numbers on this exclusive street, so I had to rely on descriptions of the landscape. Past the three palm trees by the big boulder. Past the red brick driveway. Left at the black wrought-iron gates. A flash of blue whizzed past me. *Was that our foreman's truck?* It looked like Rick's blue pickup, but I knew that was impossible. Rick just wasn't the type to be invited for tea at some rich person's home. For that matter, neither was I. *What are you doing, Kaitlin?* When I finally came to the gate that Bram described, I made a complete stop. A dead stop.

I couldn't do it.

I stared at the ornate, wrought-iron gate and felt like I did the day I learned who Bram was. My stomach churned, a constant reminder of how near the edge I was. I stared at the curling black iron, but all I could see were prison bars. Cold, ugly bars that kept my father from his family— because of the Crutchfields—and their lies. My stomach convulsed and I felt sour saliva sliding down my throat.

My Buick idled in the driveway, its hot breath sounding more like an angry lion, ready to pounce. I put the car in reverse. I *was* a Malone. I was. I didn't belong here.

"Hey! You found it!" The passenger door swung open and Bram jumped in next to me. My moment to escape had vanished. "Just go forward a little and push that button up there. The gates will swing open." My hands were frozen on the steering wheel. I swallowed hard and stared straight ahead, afraid to look into his eyes. If only my stomach would stop its roller-coaster ride.

Bram couldn't know why I sat there like a stiff mannequin. He pointed to the gate button again. "Kait? Go ahead. Just—"

My pasty tongue was suddenly unglued. "Bram! I need to talk to you. I have something I have to tell you."

Chapter 10

I SHOULD HAVE KNOWN better than to turn my head. He looked at me intently. I could see concern washing over him, his blue eyes screaming with intensity into mine. "What's wrong?" The vein near his temple pulsed. His concern was for me. Me. Kaitlin Malone. I wanted to reach out and touch the wisp that fell over one eyebrow. To reach out and run my hand along his cheek. I was crazy. It was the only explanation.

I felt the rich warm sand crumbling beneath my feet. I stepped out on the ledge, not caring how far I fell . . .

"I just wanted to tell you . . . thank you for the picture you drew of me. I wasn't sure if I ever really said thank you."

IF I HADN'T BEEN so much in awe, I probably would have been embarrassed as I parked my car next to the line of late-model cars. The house was a sprawling Mexican adobe. In spite of its rustic appearance, I could see there was not one detail left to chance: from carefully laid cobblestones on the circular drive, to full, blooming bougainvillea draping over arbors that led to mysterious gardens, to a huge fountain that bubbled in the center of the drive. Bram grabbed my bag from the backseat and led me through a courtyard into the main entrance of the house. We stopped in the living room.

"Wait here a minute. I'll be right back," Bram said, and then disappeared down a hallway. My temples pounded and I wiped my forehead. There was still time. I could still run. But maybe there weren't other Crutchfields here. Maybe it would just be Bram's friends. Through some French doors that looked out on a pool area, I could see Becky, Jason, and some other kids from school. I let out a long breath. Of course. It was only a party for teens.

I looked around the living room, and I felt the familiar Malone furrow wind its way across my brow. The Crutchfields knew nothing about peeling wallpaper or fraying blue couches. The furnishings were as carefully detailed as the outside landscape. Beautiful overstuffed couches accented with throw pillows, polished end tables that reflected vases of fresh-cut flowers, ornate tapestries on walls, all done in quiet elegance that tried to say, "Oh, we just threw a few things together," but really said, "This room cost millions of dollars, and you don't belong here, Kaitlin Malone. You can't even sit on the edge of one of our couches. Go home to your sagging porch." I hated them. Not because of their things, but because of their shallowness. They were horrible, ugly people who didn't know how they had made my dad suffer. Only Bram was different. My eyes continued to wander and stopped at a table across the room. A dozen pictures in a variety of frames rested on it. My eyes were immediately drawn to one in the middle of them all. Robert Crutchfield. The only Crutchfield I had ever seen besides Bram. It wasn't the picture I had seen a hundred times on the news, but a casual picture of him, his hair tossed by the wind, a gentle smile on his lips. I looked away.

"Kait?"

I whipped around, startled by the soft voice. A woman with shoulder-length blond hair was reaching out and taking my hand into hers. Bram stood next to her.

"It's very nice to meet you. Bram has talked about you so much. I'm his mother, Allison Crutchfield."

I felt her squeezing my hand. It was warm and smooth. There were no claws, no scales as my childhood mind had imagined. She was an attractive woman. Her smile was genuine, her manner open. Her eyes rested on my face, and I waited for her to shriek with recognition. I waited for her to pull a gun from a drawer and shoot me dead. But she didn't. She was welcoming me into her home, putting her arm around my shoulder and guiding me out to the patio for a soda. I felt like I was watching a movie. It wasn't really me doing all these things. She asked me about school.

"Bram tells me you are quite the student. All AP classes." She smiled as she jerked her head toward Bram. "I wish some of that would rub off on him."

Bram rolled his eyes. "Oh, let's not go there."

"Well, all of my classes aren't AP. I also have a local history class."

"Really!" she said. "You might be interested in browsing through a bunch of old boxes I have out in the garage."

"Oh, c'mon, Mom," Bram moaned, as he opened a can of Coke. "I don't think she's going to want to look through our old photo albums. You can't even get *me* to do that."

"Photo albums?" I asked.

"No," she said, shaking her head. "He doesn't know what he's talking about. There's a few old pictures, but it's mostly old letters, maps, bills—I'm not really even sure. I brought them over from the old farmhouse a couple of years ago to sort through the stuff. The Twin Oaks Historical Society asked for early documents from our area, but I didn't just want to hand everything over until I had a chance to look through it. Shortly after I had them brought to our garage—" She stopped and looked at Bram. "Well, I just didn't get a chance to look through them for different reasons, but I'm sure there is some interesting local history in there."

"What do you mean?" I asked.

"Well, some of the stuff dates back to the first Crutchfields on this land—Maggie Crutchfield. She kept diaries and records of everything. Did you know she was one of the founders of Twin Oaks?"

Founder? Founder! I felt my Malone blood boil. *Right! You mean one of the traitors, losers, lowlifes. God!* Wasn't she embarrassed to even bring up her name? I was embarrassed for Bram to have Maggie for an ancestor. It was the Malones who gave Twin Oaks its name. The *Malones*— not the Crutchfields. Amanda and Jared Malone planted an oak tree for each of their children when they were born. The ancient oaks still graced the entrance to our property. I wondered if *she* knew that.

"No, I didn't know that," I finally answered.

"Yes, she was quite a woman. And a writer of sorts, too—at least that is what I would guess by all the diaries and letters she wrote. She even had a few poems published in the local paper."

"Maggie...kept journals?" I asked.

"Well, I guess you could call them that."

"Yeah, Kait, sort of like you," Bram chimed in.

No! Not like me. She was nothing like me. She couldn't be.

"Oh, you write, Kait? Then you really should browse through the boxes. Bram, why don't you take her out to the garage later—after the others leave? You're welcome to borrow anything out there."

"Thank you," I said quietly, but I had no intention of reading anything written by Maggie Crutchfield.

Allison Crutchfield grabbed my hand, squeezing it

again, and she looked into my eyes and smiled. "Bram's right. You are a very nice girl. You're always welcome in our home."

I returned her gaze. I wanted to hate her. I had planned to hate her, and thought I might be able to when she brought up Maggie, but it wasn't working. When I looked into her face, I saw a gentle woman. Where were the evil Crutchfields?

Bram excused us and we walked out to the pool area, where the others were. We looked like a couple as we approached, and I wondered if we were. But really, other than the wild fantasies in my head, Bram had only said he thought I was someone he could be good friends with. Maybe that was all we were.

"Hey, here they come," Matt bellowed.

They. Even that word made my arms tingle. I hoped we were a "they."

"Bram! Looks like you're still dry. We'll have to fix that," Jason said. He and Matt grabbed Bram's arms and after a wild scuffle, all three fell into the pool—clothes and all. Becky was the next target, then Jenny. A couple of boys I hadn't met yet jumped in to avoid being dragged. I edged away from the commotion, but it didn't do any good. Bram and Jason came after me, and though I wished they would have at least let me kick my shoes off, I was soon laughing and swimming in the pool with the rest. After that we feasted on burgers, hot dogs, salads, and brownies, served by what I assume was a maid. Again, no detail was overlooked. Piles of dry towels were brought for us to wrap up in as we lay around on the multitude of lounge chairs that surrounded the pool. We laughed about our classes, our teachers, and the endless ways freshmen annoyed seniors. As the sun went down, lights in the surrounding landscape magically lit up, and the warm evening breeze stirred up the sweet jasmine, its intoxicating scent sending me further into this dream world. I lay back on the lounge chair and stared into the black sky, sparkling with unknown worlds.

A galaxy away, a universe away, a world spins, and I fly through light-years to explore it. Light-years that may erase the life I had on my own small planet, but as I travel, the old planet fades into a forgotten galaxy. The sparkling blackness, the mystery beyond, seduces me . . .

I breathed in deeply.

I *was* Kait Hampton.

I felt like I could be Kait Hampton forever.

Chapter 11

"WATCH OUT. There might be skeletons in some of those."

"That's what I'm hoping," I said, as I slid the latch across on an old trunk inscribed with chipped gold letters. MAGGIE CRUTCHFIELD.

I was indeed doing what I said I had no intention of doing. When the party began to break up and Bram walked people out to their cars, I gathered up my things to leave, too. As the last car disappeared down the drive, I opened my car door. Bram stood beside me, nervously tapping his fingers on the rusty roof. I thought it was the moment of truth. Were we just friends, or something more? Suddenly he pounded his hand on the roof.

"Hey! The boxes! Didn't you want to look at those?"

He remembered the boxes in the garage and insisted we go take a look. He didn't have to twist my arm. I was even willing to look at Maggie Crutchfield's dusty memories if it meant the evening would last longer. Another hour in my dream world with Bram.

"Wow! This is so cool!" Bram lifted an old moth-eaten coat from the trunk he was sifting through. "I didn't know there would be stuff like this."

I hesitated near another trunk. I was afraid to lift the lid. I was afraid Maggie Crutchfield would reach out with her bony fingers and choke me. It was crazy. She had been dead for nearly a century, but she had always been so present in our lives. Her treachery still affected us.

Bram slipped on the old coat with brass buttons and dug deeper into the trunk, emerging with a saber. "Looks like we had a soldier in the family." He held a goofy pose that made me laugh. He rummaged a little more and then grunted. "Nothing else good in here. Just a bunch of old papers. History's never been one of my favorite subjects. Who cares what happened in the past?"

I felt encouraged. Maybe this was my chance to come clean. I turned and faced him. "What about bad things that happened in the past? Do you care about that?"

Bram took off the coat and threw it back in the trunk. "Whew! It's hot in here!" I saw the vein near his temple bulge, his jaw tighten. He didn't answer me.

He cared. The past mattered.

I turned back to the trunk and kneeled down in front

of it. My throat felt like it was swelling. There were some things that could never be forgotten.

Bram would never forget his father was dead.

I would never forget that a good, kind, gentle man was behind bars. I would never forget the image of my father sobbing in my mother's arms, jerked awake by the nightmare of the night he and Robert Crutchfield argued. And I would never, ever forget the chilling silence when my mother returned home from the courtroom, alone, and silently shut her bedroom door behind her.

My vision began to blur. *Don't cry, you stupid idiot! Don't you dare!* The silence grew louder. Bram's hatred ran so deep he couldn't even speak about it...How long would I have to remain Kaitlin Hampton?

I threw open the lid of the trunk. I would rather face the suffocating hand of Maggie than the hatred of Bram. There were no bony hands reaching for my throat. Some crumbling brown paper filled the top with a fraying, thin satin ribbon holding the bulk of it together. Where the paper was torn away, I could see a delicately crocheted blanket with a blue ribbon woven through the edging. A baby blanket.

My fingers shook as I reached in to feel the fabric. It was still soft after decades of being forgotten. Soft enough that I could imagine the baby it once held. It made me shiver. Something was wrong with this picture. It was too tender. I tugged on the ancient satin ribbon and pulled away the rest of the paper. I scooped the blanket into my arms and laid it against my cheek. I heard a gentle weeping as I nestled in closer to the soft fabric. And then I felt the wet tears that had been stored up for a century running down my cheeks. And when Bram dropped to his knees beside me, I realized the sobs were my own.

"Kait. Kait, what is it?" He pulled the blanket away from my hands, perhaps thinking that a ghost from the past was pricking me . . . and maybe it was. He cupped my face in his hands, and I stared past his eyes into what seemed his soul. I prayed he could not see into mine. He slowly leaned forward and kissed the tears from my cheek. My skin burned and I found it was difficult to breathe, but then his lips traveled across my face and found my mouth, and I forgot about breathing at all.

Chapter 12

THUMPITY-THUMPITY-THUMPITY...

I veered the car back into my lane. It was dangerous for me to be driving. Only the occasional blinding headlight or the bumps on the road brought me back to my vinyl seat and the warm summer wind blowing through my hair. Otherwise, I was in another world, on another planet, in a blissfully different universe, with Bram's hand running down my back, his breath breathing an unearthly beat in my ear, his lips sliding down my neck, across my shoulder...

Thumpity-thumpity-thumpity...

Breathe, Kaitlin, breathe. Keep your eyes on the road, for God's sake!

But even now, my breaths were ragged. I relived every moment that Bram held me, touched me, kissed me. My back burned where he had pulled me closer, my skin still did a wild dance where he had brushed it with his lips, and my eyes completely lost focus when I remembered his words whispered in my ear. Every word—every syllable was pushing me to the brink of insanity, I was sure. Was it a dream? Had he really whispered those things as he followed the curve of my neck? I heard the words again.

"Kaitlin, I've dreamed about you every night since the first day I saw you...I knew someday I would meet someone like you...Kaitlin...I know this is crazy...I don't know how it could happen...but I love you...I love you."

And it was crazy. Bram was as certifiable as me. Complete strangers just didn't fall in love in two weeks' time. I didn't believe in love at first sight. It was a myth. But I had repeated the words back to Bram—and I meant them. How was I to know? I had never been in love before, but whatever it was, I knew I would do anything to protect it.

So now I wondered, how long could I go on with this masquerade? How long would it be before he stumbled upon my name? A chance look at my driver's license? An accidental slip on a school paper? How long before we bumped into another friend like Becky, who knew who I really was? How long before Abby was convinced of my betrayal and blew the whistle? There were so many things that could go wrong...so many tangled complications that could ruin everything between me and Bram.

It was a time bomb ticking, and I had more to lose now than ever. How long could I keep pretending? The answer was simple—as long as it took. However long it took for Bram to accept me as Kaitlin Malone.

My lies would have to be good. Better than good. They had to be flawless. I had almost slipped when I held the baby blanket up to my face. I didn't know I was going to cry—I wasn't even sure *why* I was crying—at least not then. And that turned out to be good, because when Bram asked me why I was crying, I just shook my head and didn't answer. He seemed to understand. But now I knew what yanked my tears from unknown depths. Fear. Complete, utter fear, like I was hanging on the edge of a cliff and finger by finger a hand was pushing me off.

First Bram, then his mother, and finally a baby blanket lovingly packed away by a young mother. Maggie Crutchfield, like the other Crutchfields, was becoming something I didn't want her to be—human.

I glanced at the seat next to me. Her ancient diary lay there. I had slipped it from the trunk before I left and asked Bram if I could borrow it. It was my last hope. If I couldn't find the evil Maggie Crutchfield in there, then I might as well become Kaitlin Hampton. I would have no reason to be a Malone.

WHEN I GOT HOME the house was dark, except for a small night-light shining in the living room, but I shoved the diary beneath my shirt anyway and climbed our creaky stairs. Each groaning step pounded in my ears.

"Kaitlin? That you?"

I clutched the hidden diary closer to my chest. "Yeah, Mom. I'm home."

"Good. Good night, honey."

"Night." I looked at Abby's open door. I knew if she was awake, she would hear the fear in my voice. If she turned on her light, she would see it in my face. More fuel for her suspicions. But all was quiet from her room. In my bedroom I moved around in the darkness, still afraid to turn on a light. I slid the diary under my bed and balled some old sweatpants on top of it. The house was still. I finally let out a long, slow breath and crawled between my cool sheets. If there was truth—or lies—in the diary, it would have to wait until later.

Tonight was the night I learned we were a "they," and I was going to savor every minute of it.

Chapter 13

"HOW DO I LOOK?" I asked.

"You look like someone who is going to be in deep ca-ca if Bram doesn't get here soon." Becky picked a stray hair from my shirt. "Remember who really lives here? My parents are going to be home in fifteen minutes."

The knot that had taken up residence in my stomach the last few weeks twisted a little tighter. I stared at the clock, feeling slightly hysterical that Bram was late. When my excuses for meeting him places had finally run dry and he insisted on picking me up at my house, I had finally conceded and given him Becky's address. Now I stood near the front door like it was my own, pretending I lived on Juniper Avenue. "I don't know how much longer I can keep this up, Becky."

"Then don't, Kait! What are you waiting for? Bram is nuts about you. He's not going to care that you're a Malone."

"Becky, knowing someone for a little over a month can't wipe out what you've believed for a lifetime. You just don't know how it's been between them and us."

"I know how it is between him and you *now* though. That's what counts. You were right, Kaitlin. It *is* more than 'the hots.' I see it every time he looks at you. You two were meant for each other. Give the guy some credit."

Becky just didn't know how it was. I did give Bram credit. We had spent every spare moment with each other ever since that night in his garage. But the closer we got, the more I felt I had to lose. Instead of getting easier, it became harder to tell the truth. And there was one "small" detail that Becky forgot.

"Becky, I know Bram is the most understanding, caring person in the world . . . but, my father did—" I couldn't say the words aloud.

"Kill his father?"

I nodded. "Even if it was an accident, would *you* be able to forget that?"

"I think more than that is bothering you. I think deep down, you still don't trust the Crutchfields—even Bram. You won't admit it, not even to yourself, but I think this is your way of keeping some distance from him—just in case it turns out that he does bite."

I rolled my eyes up to the ceiling. "Well, thank you, Dr. Becky. And when did you get your degree in psychology? You can send me your bill." But I knew the truth when I heard it, and there was a grain of truth in Becky's words. I was still afraid of the Crutchfields. How could I not be? It was all I had ever known. And there was still the matter of their lies that had put my father in prison. My father hadn't murdered Robert Crutchfield as they had claimed. It was an accident, pure and simple. My father had told me so. I knew Bram was different, and his mother seemed nice, too, but tonight I would meet other Crutchfields. Maybe they were the ones I had always been warned about. "Thanks for the analysis, Beck, but I'm doing the best I can."

Becky sighed. "So what are you going to do? Lie forever? It's only a matter of time, you know, before he finds out. Jeez, Jason knows where I live. If he and Bram ever start comparing notes..."

The knot in my stomach doubled, and I felt my eyes sting.

"Jeez Louise! Don't start clouding up on me! You don't have time to fix your mascara!" Becky wrapped her arms around me and hugged me tight. "It will be okay. Just don't cry! I hate that!"

I smiled and nodded. "I'm not wearing any mascara anyway."

Becky pushed me away and rolled her eyes. "Oh, you make me sick! A hunk of a boyfriend and thick lashes, too!"

We heard a car door slam, and I rushed to the narrow window that bordered Becky's front door. It was Bram.

"Okay. I'm going to hide," Becky said. "When he

rings the bell, answer the door, grab your purse, and go!" Becky glanced at her watch. "Don't chitchat unless you want to introduce your 'new' mom and dad."

"Thanks, Becky. We'll hurry."

Becky ran up the stairs to her bedroom, and I took a last look in the hall mirror. I could see guilt all over my face. I wondered why Bram never saw it.

The bell rang, and I opened the door.

"Hi. Let me just grab—"

Bram stepped inside and lowered his lips to mine. His hand gently caressed my cheek.

"Gosh, I've missed you."

It was Sunday. We had spent Saturday night together, Friday night together, and every day at school before that. I smiled. "I've missed you, too. Let me grab my purse and we'll go."

"Are your parents here?" he whispered. "Can I meet them?"

"No!" The word burst from my lips. *Steady, girl.* "I mean, they're not home. Nobody's home. Sorry." The phone rang. The bubbling acid in my stomach erupted. I snatched my purse from the hall chair. "I'm ready!"

"Aren't you going to get the phone?" Bram asked.

"Oh, the machine will get it. Let's just go." The ringing continued.

Like in a dream, Bram's feet seemed to be stuck to the floor, and no matter how hard I tried, I couldn't seem to get him out the door. I heard the click of the machine turning on. My God! We could hear the recorded voice in the kitchen all the way out to the hallway. I ran, knowing each word brought me closer to disaster.

"Hi. We can't take your call right now but leave a message for Paul, Anne, B—"

I yanked the receiver from the hook. "Hello!" I yelled.

"Hello? Becky? Is that you?"

I could tell Lisa, Becky's sister, was confused. She expected her sister to be answering the phone, not me. I was about to whisper into the phone, but then saw Bram come up behind me.

"Uh, no. She's not here right now. Can I take a message?" This was crazy. I was going to fall off this tightrope any moment. Bram stood there listening to every word of the one-sided conversation, kissing the fingers of my free hand, one by one.

"Kait? That you? What are you doing at our house if Becky's not there?"

"She's in the bathroom. Can you call back in five minutes?"

"Sure. Bye." Lisa hung up, and I replaced the receiver.

"I thought you said no one was home," Bram said.

I shrugged. "Only my sister. Practically the same as no one." I was getting good at this game. The words came fast, like they were almost the truth. I almost believed they were. The line between truth and lies didn't seem as distinct anymore.

We left without any further disasters, and once we were in Bram's territory, on his fancy street, in his fancy house, walking through his fancy yard, I was able to relax.

There wasn't a trace of my other life here to catch me up. The setting helped me to relax, too. The lawns, pathways, nooks, grottoes, and gardens were all perfectly manicured. It was almost eerie, like every stray leaf was magically sucked out of sight. Not like my house, where a walk around the property produced a mental checklist of everything that needed to be done. Weeds, painting, repairs, hauling. There were some good things about being a Crutchfield.

"Shouldn't we go back and see if your mom needs any help?" I asked. When we walked through the house, his mother was busy putting up decorations for Josh's fifth birthday party. He had already had a party with his friends, but tonight was just for family—and me.

"Oh, she'll call us if she needs us," Bram said.

"But we'll never hear her way out here." We had stopped at a gazebo down a steep, sloped path at the end of their property. It looked out across a canyon and to the rest of Twin Oaks beyond. I could even see the green and brown Malone hills in the distance.

"I've got my beeper. She knows how to use it." Bram smiled and pulled me down beside him on the bench in the gazebo. He pointed out to the distant hills. "See that little white dot way out there?"

I squinted my eyes and followed the line of his hand. I couldn't see a white dot. "No."

He pulled me closer and pointed again. "Right there."

I saw the white dot just a little to the left of the Malone property. I knew what it was. "Yes, I see it now."

"That's the original Crutchfield farmhouse. My mom has been busy restoring it. I think she's going to give it to the Twin Oaks Historical Society or something like that. It's got to be a hundred years old."

Actually it's a hundred and twenty years old, Bram, and it's not the original farmhouse. Mine is the original farmhouse. But I just said, "Oh."

"And see that little strip of land just above it? It's about all we have left of the original Crutchfield farmland. Part of it even looks out to the ocean. I go up there sometimes and draw. It's about the most peaceful place in the world."

"I'd like to go there someday with you."

"Yeah, that would be good," he said, nodding his head. "It may not be empty too much longer."

"What do you mean?"

"I think my uncle is finally going ahead with my dad's dream for a retreat there. For years my dad and him wanted to build it, but I guess to do it right they needed a little bit more of the land to the north to widen the road leading to it. They made lots of offers on the land, but in the past the owners wouldn't sell."

"And the owners are selling now?"

"Not yet. But things may be changing soon."

Not likely. I knew the land he was talking about, and the many offers the Crutchfield lawyers had made. The Crutchfields just didn't get it. We wouldn't sell. Ever. Especially not to them.

We stared out at the thin wispy clouds that were just beginning to turn pink around the edges as the sun moved closer to the horizon. We sat there in silence, much the same way we did in the courtyard at school as I wrote in my journal and Bram drew in his sketchbook. Bram had given me several more drawings since the first one. A few were of me, a few were of groups of friends chatting, unaware they were being sketched. Bram captured with lines what I tried to capture with words. I could see the coyness of Jenny talking to Matt, the bravado of Jason as he told a story, the shyness of Lexie, a new girl who followed Jenny around like a lost puppy. His drawings didn't make fun of them, they were just . . . honest. His drawings of me were honest, too. I tried to imagine what he was thinking as he studied me—I even asked him one day as I looked at a drawing, the shadows creeping across my face with an evasive hint of sadness. He had shrugged. "I was just trying to catch another side of you—one that's hidden most of the time, but sometimes I can see it, maybe feel it. I'm learning more and more about you, Kaitlin Hampton. Watch out!" He laughed. I didn't.

I also learned that I wasn't the only one he amazed with his drawings. Jenny told me he had won every award there was for his drawings, both in and out of school. She called him a "rare talent."

I looked from the pink-tinged sky to Bram's profile, studying the landscape with his artist's eye. "Bram, why did you change your plans about going to the Design Institute? Surely your family can afford it."

Bram laughed, but it was an empty laugh, just air coming up from his lungs. "Gosh, Kait, if the problem were only money, I'd be out there digging ditches or whatever I had to do to get there. Money wouldn't be my problem."

"Then what's keeping you?"

He just sat there. I could tell he was searching for the right words. His eyes scanned the sky and finally came to rest in a vacant stare at his feet. "Me. It's just me."

"But you love to draw. You live and breathe it. Why wouldn't you want to study it more? You have a gift, Bram."

He swallowed hard and shook his head. "I always dreamed about studying at the Design Institute. A couple of years ago I even sent away for an application. I finally got the nerve up one night to show my dad. He never really thought of my art as a future—just a nice little hobby. We had a big fight about it." Bram and I could talk about anything, but whenever he started talking about his dead father, I felt like a spy. I felt every drop of the Malone blood that flowed through my veins, and more than anything else in the world, I wanted to blurt out who I was— but the coward in me let him go on. "He said I could do art in my spare time, but in college I should study business . . . because that is what the Crutchfields do." Bram laughed his empty laugh again. I wanted to reach out and hold him, squeeze him so tight he forgot about everything but me.

"Bram, every kid has arguments with their parents. Don't let that keep you from your dream."

"It wasn't just any argument, Kait. It was our last argument. He died that night."

I stood up and walked to the rail of the gazebo. I didn't want to hear this. I didn't want Bram to see my face and capture with his artist's eye the guilt that lurked there. I didn't say anything, hoping the pain in his own voice would choke him and stop him. But it didn't. He went on.

"I had just said, 'Screw Crutchfield Enterprises!' when the phone rang. My dad grabbed the phone and talked to the foreman of a business park he was developing. There was a terrible storm that night and a mud slide was threatening a pumping station near there. The only way they could prevent disaster was to move some heavy equipment in . . ."

Bram continued, but I knew the story from there. I remember looking out from our rain-pelted living-room window and seeing the lights of the bulldozers in the distance, moving across our property. I remember my dad cursing and saying they weren't going to mow over our tomato fields to save their buildings. "It's their own damn fault they didn't leave enough access. I knew this would happen someday." I remember my mom grabbing my dad's arm as he went toward the front door, saying we should just call the police. "The police are in the Crutchfields' hip pocket, too. A lot of damn good that'll do!" He stormed out, and that was the last time I saw my father as a free man. Bram and I both lost something that night.

I turned and faced him. I was tired of being a coward. "Bram—"

"Kait, don't you see? Usually my dad would have just told the foreman to handle it. My dad wore a business

87

suit. He wasn't the type to tromp around muddy hills in the middle of the night. But he was so pumped up, so angry at me, that he just stomped out of the house that night." Bram's eyes glistened, and at that moment I felt like my bones were being sucked right out of me. My legs felt limp. "It was my fault that—" His voice cracked.

I ran over to him, dropping to my knees and lifting his face with my hands. "Don't! Don't ever say that! Please, Bram!" We didn't say another word. We just held each other and that was enough, and then his beeper finally buzzed and we walked back to the house.

Chapter 14

THE HOUSE WAS FULL of commotion when we walked back in through the French doors to the dining room. Besides Bram's mother, Josh, and Bram's middle brother, Ty, nearly a dozen other people filled the room. I tensed up, not expecting so many relatives, fearful that maybe one of them would recognize me as a Malone. Bram began introducing me to them. I met Aunt Barb, the twins, three other cousins, ancient Uncle Cecil and his not-so-ancient wife, Sherry, and Aunt Teresa, who quietly sipped a large glass of clear brown liquid in the corner of the room. Perhaps she was the twins' mother. I wasn't sure. I was just relieved that everyone smiled at me when I met them. No one knew who they really shook hands with.

"Where's Uncle Jack?" Bram asked his mom.

"Out in the kitchen, I think."

Bram grabbed my hand and dragged me to the kitchen. A tall, dark-haired man was pouring himself a glass of wine at the kitchen counter when we walked in. When he lifted his eyes, I was startled. They were the same golden yellow as mine. An unusual color I rarely saw. All of the other Crutchfields were blond and blue eyed.

"Kait, this is my uncle Jack."

Uncle Jack noticed the similarity, too, I was sure. He paused and looked at me for a few seconds before saying anything. And it wasn't just the color of our eyes—our hair, our cheekbones, even our lips were similar. Was it possible for genes to travel through that many generations?

He held his hand out to me. "So this is the famous Kait Hampton. It's nice to meet you at last." I felt my cheeks grow hot and looked at Bram as I held my hand out.

Bram shrugged and smiled. "So I guess I may have mentioned you a few times."

Uncle Jack took my hand and wouldn't let go. He looked into my eyes and didn't say anything. He seemed to be studying me, his face somber. My heart pounded, and in a fleeting second my brain knew why. *He knows! Oh, my God! He knows! Not here! Not now!* I was frozen, but my mind raced at how I would explain it all to Bram. That is, if all the Crutchfields didn't kill me first.

He released his grip on my hand. "She is beautiful, just like you said, Bram."

I felt dizzy, giddy, and Bram's and Uncle Jack's words became distant echoes as I realized how paranoid I had become. *Steady, Kait. Steady.*

"Bram tells me you came all the way from Las Vegas for Josh's birthday," I said.

"Well, I have to admit, I'm here on some business, too. Even though I oversee Crutchfield holdings in Vegas, I needed to come out and help Allison with a—" He paused, looked at Bram, and then continued, "—with some unfinished business. Right, Bram?"

I saw Bram's cheek twitch, and one corner of his mouth pulled down into a frown. He flicked the wine cork laying on the counter with his finger, and it shot across the room, startling his cat over in the corner. "C'mon," he said. "Let's go back with the others." Bram obviously didn't like to talk about business, finished or unfinished, and I wondered if it was because it was the obstacle to his art.

We went back in with the others, and the rest of the evening was normal. Normal. Oh, his family had their quirky sides. Aunt Teresa drank too much, ancient Uncle Cecil's jokes were too raw and Sherry kept shushing him and then laughing this squeaky little laugh, and Aunt Barb rolled her eyes at Sherry when she wasn't looking. But everyone sang as Josh blew out his candles. Everyone ate their cake and remembered back to this birthday or that. Everyone sat on their chairs, or looked out the window, or got up to go to the bathroom—in a very normal way. They were just a family, like any other, and my hope that tonight I might meet the evil Crutchfields vanished.

"Bram, would you mind taking me home?" It was only eight-thirty and the party was still going strong, but my head ached and I was suddenly so tired.

Bram dropped me off at Becky's house and I waved from the sidewalk until his car turned the corner, and then I got in my car to drive to my real home. My mom was surprised I was home before nine o'clock, and Abby asked why I spent so much time at Becky's. She put extra emphasis on Becky's name. She was always digging. Abby's comment jogged my mom's memory.

"Well, don't make any plans for this coming Friday. Remember... your dad comes home." Her voice sounded excited, but her face showed her worry. We were all nervous. How had prison changed him?

"I remember," I said, and I climbed the stairs to the bathroom. I opened our medicine cabinet and took out a bottle of aspirin. I popped two in my mouth and swished away the bitter taste with a handful of water, then splashed some water from the chipped rust-stained sink onto my face. I looked at my image in the mirror and wasn't sure who I saw: Kaitlin Hampton or Kaitlin Malone. I rubbed my hand across my forehead, searching for the angry furrow my grandmother had passed on to me. It had been there just a month ago.

I breathed in a long, ragged breath and let it out slowly. There was still Maggie Crutchfield. The evil had to be somewhere. I believed my parents. I trusted them. The stories had to come from somewhere. I had been afraid to look at her diary, and it was still hidden under my bed, but I wasn't afraid anymore. I went to my room and quietly shut the door. My balled-up sweats were still lying on top of the diary. I pulled it out and lay down on my bed to read it.

"Please, please, don't let this be a lie, too," I whispered. I needed Maggie to be the slut I had always believed she was. I opened the diary and saw delicately scrolled handwriting. I carefully turned the brittle, yellow pages. The handwriting was beautiful, but difficult to read.

December 18, 1879
I have spent the fuller part of a week in the house now. The rain has come with a vengeance, and I am sentenced to changing pails where Mr. Henley's crafts-manship is lacking. I intend to pay him a visit as soon as the roads dry. My only solace in being stranded is that the book I sent for, Pride and Prejudice, *arrived and I am able to read it without interruption. I have read it thrice now, and will yet again. I laugh and weep each time.*

I could relate to the leaking roof. I was more than familiar with stepping around buckets during the rainy season. But this entry still gave no insight into the evil Maggie Crutchfield, just someone dealing with the nuisances of life, and a glimpse of someone who enjoyed reading—like me. I skimmed through the pages searching for something more revealing. There were entries about the price of barley, her hopes for a nearby train station, her complaints about the carpenters who finished her new home, the beauty of the wild mustard covering the springtime hills, but there didn't seem to be anything about her numerous affairs with men or her selling off of the Crutchfield land. I stopped at a page where a tiny flower had been pressed between the pages. Its petals were faded; a faint hint of purple fanned out from its center. I guessed it might be a violet.

April 22, 1880
I completed the planting of my spring garden today. Mrs. Willets scolded me, protesting a woman of my condition should not be tilling the ground. I must confess that with the weight I bear, I feared I might not rise again from my knees, but I had resolved I should have flowers in June. I will need flowers in June. If not for myself, then as a symbol to others that joy still resides in this house.

I wondered at the significance of June and who she was trying to impress, but putting on a show for the neighbors didn't exactly sound evil. She loved flowers. My mother always planted a small flower garden, too—except for this last year. I continued to skim. Finally, on the last page was an entry that made me slow down and read every word—an entry mentioning her baby. I remembered the carefully wrapped blanket in the trunk.

June 7, 1880
The babe hardly moves at all now, but the dear Lord knows there is scarce little room. I am so large with

this precious child. It could be any day now, which brings me great joy, aside from the sadness of being so alone. Of course, I have secured a woman from San Diego to reside with me and she is experienced with such matters, but, still, there is no family, no one close to announce, "Another Crutchfield has been born." Yes, he will share my name, the Crutchfield name, since the father refuses to acknowledge his fit of desire. This wounds me deeply, but the cruelest blow is to see Amanda, pushing her new babe in a pram, her head held high, while she expects me to hang mine in shame. Of course, I was wrong to give in to his seductions, his flattery, to betray my own sister, and I have begged forgiveness, but she has none for me. Perhaps someday my weakness will be forgiven. But my child will not suffer because of my folly. One way or another, he shall be able to hold his head up high in this community. Even my sister and her cowardly husband shall not prevent that, despite the lies they spread about my character to cover their own shame. Jared Malone may not acknowledge his own child, but I promise, I swear, my child will not suffer because of it.

I stopped and reread the last sentence. Jared Malone was the father of Maggie's baby? Jared *Malone*? She was lying! She had to be! But the truth had already settled in my belly like a throbbing ulcer. I closed the diary and stared at the peeling wallpaper on my bedroom wall.

"It was a lie." My bare whisper seemed to boom through the silent room. "It was all . . . always a lie."

The treachery had not just been Maggie's, but the Malones' as well. If Maggie Crutchfield was a slut, then Jared Malone was a slimy cheat. My whole life was a lie. Our reason for scrimping, scraping, shunning so many of the conveniences built on Crutchfield land, never selling one acre of Malone land, was because we were better than they were. We had integrity—or we thought we did.

I leaned over and switched off my bedroom light. I felt more than a century of lies clawing their way up my throat, choking me. Two sisters and their foolish pride had left a horrible legacy of hatred behind them. Their lies and betrayal hadn't died with them but had taken on a life of their own with their children, and their children's children. Becky's words that night in the bathroom at Red's flashed through my mind . . . *Oh, what a tangled web we weave . . .*

I rolled over and shoved my face into my pillow. My muffled sobs were unlike any I had ever cried. Deathly moans that frightened me, but they wouldn't stop, and I cried and cried until I felt empty.

I was empty. And in a strange way, it felt good.

Chapter 15

I READ MAGGIE'S diaries every day after that. I had called Bram the next morning before school and asked him to bring them all with him. "I really need them, Bram," I said. "For my local history class. It would really help me out." Another lie, but I hardly cared anymore. To me, it seemed the only way to get at the truth. I had to know everything about where I came from. Where my father came from, Bram's father, everything that made us who we are, because I really didn't know anymore.

And I knew now, it wasn't a matter of *when* I was going to tell Bram, but *if.* I had lost my edge. I had always thought the Malones were better than "them." Secretly, I had thought that one day Bram would see this. He would see it and understand. Then I would tell him. But now we were the "them."

So now the question was "if." It was insane, but I pictured us ten years from now, twenty years, even thirty years when we were old and gray, and I was still hiding out at Becky's, and even though Bram and I were married and had children and grandchildren, I was still Kaitlin Hampton to him.

I loved Bram. It wasn't "the hots" or puppy love. It was love, and I wasn't embarrassed to admit it anymore. He was the only *real* thing in my life. And there was no way I was going to ruin it, even if it meant I had to lie forever. In the meantime, I read everything I could about Maggie Crutchfield. I wanted to know about Amanda and Jared, too, but they didn't leave any written record, so Maggie was my only key to the past. Someday I needed to be able to explain to Bram about the real history of our families. Though I never heard him or his family mention the Malones, I knew he was raised to hate them just as I hated the Crutchfields—or used to hate them. I had to somehow give him time to change his mind about us, too. And most important of all, I had to somehow make him believe that his father's death was an accident.

October 14

A crumbling illusion is a frightening thing. It frees some. It buries and suffocates others. And the cruelest thing is, we never know which we shall be—the one riding to freedom or the one gasping for a last breath.

"Kaitlin Malone?"

I looked up from my journal, startled, and glanced around the counselor's office waiting room to see if anyone I knew was around. Apparently all of my records weren't changed—only the ones for the attendance. The counselor was "in" on our little secret—too bad the secretary wasn't. Luckily, all those waiting around me were strangers. No one flinched at my name. I closed my journal and went into Mrs. Flannery's office. It was my senior appointment. All seniors had them in the fall to make sure all their paperwork and classes were in order to graduate and go on to college. Except I wasn't going to college, so I figured my appointment would be quite short. The Malones couldn't afford to fix a sagging porch, much less pay for college tuition. Besides, my dad had been preparing me for the tomato business since I could walk through a newly plowed field. It was already decided that I would take a few business and computer courses at the community college, and the rest he and my mom would teach me. Someday I would be running the Malone Company. I had the rusty keys hanging on my bedpost to prove it. I remember Abby's face when my dad gave me the keys. They had hung on his bedpost forever, and one day he just walked into the living room and handed them to me. They were nothing but a bunch of old rusty keys on a huge rusty ring, and they didn't open a single thing on our property—but they once had. And that was all that mattered. The Malones didn't have a fancy crest, but the keys were our symbol that we were somebody. We had traditions we didn't forget. They had always hung on a Malone bedpost. Now they would hang on mine. Rusty keys and the sacredness of our land went hand in hand. But Abby always wanted the keys to hang in her room. I knew by the tightness of her lips, the lowering of her eyelids—her silence—when Dad handed them to me.

"My goodness, Kaitlin!" Mrs. Flannery said as she went through my folder. "It takes a lot to impress me, but I will admit, I am impressed. I don't think you need to worry about graduating." She ruffled some more through my folder. ". . . and it looks here like you already took the SAT."

"Yes. Everyone at Holy Trinity had to take it."

She looked up at me and smiled. "So where do you plan on applying to college?"

"I'm not."

Her smiled faded. "What?"

"I'm not going to college."

"I heard what you said, Kaitlin, but I don't understand. Between your GPA, SAT scores, and the course work you've taken, you could get into any college you wanted—*any* college."

"But colleges take money, Mrs. Flannery, and *that* I don't have." I was annoyed that she would assume all Twin Oaks seniors were dripping in money.

"Well, Kaitlin, dear, there are all kinds of student loans and scholarships to help—"

"No, Mrs. Flannery, you don't understand. I mean *no* money."

She looked back inside my folder and flipped through

the papers. She finally looked up. "I see here you've received a lot of recognition for your writing. Looks like you show a lot of promise there. Did you know there are colleges that offer full scholarships for students with your talent and academic success?"

"What do you mean, full scholarships?" I was embarrassed that I knew so little about colleges and scholarships, but since I already had my future planned out, I never looked into it.

"Full means everything. Room and board, and tuition. Some even include a small amount of spending money, if you qualify. Here, let me punch some information into the computer, and I can give you a printout of which colleges might be right for you. It would be a shame to waste your talents, Kaitlin." She began typing on her computer.

I knew I should stop her. Tell her it was a big waste of time. My parents needed me to help with the family business. I didn't need college. My future was already planned. But now I said the word in my head. *College.* College. It seemed like my very own original thought. And I thought about how I felt when I wrote my stories or jotted down thoughts in my journal, and I wondered...just wondered...

But I was a Malone with some rusty keys hanging on my bedpost. I could hear the way my father jingled them the day he handed them to me.

"Thanks, Mrs. Flannery, but you don't need to bother. Like I said, it's not part of the plan." I grabbed my backpack and left.

Chapter 16

IT WAS BETWEEN CLASSES, so the halls were empty and quiet as I returned to class, but soon I heard footsteps behind me. I glanced over my shoulder. It was the Bookends. What were they both doing out of class? I picked up my pace, and so did they.

"Hey, Kaitlin, wait up."

The stupid twits. Didn't they get the idea? Was I going to have to flick their hats again? I figured they were dense and it was best to ignore them, so I walked a little faster. They stayed right on my heels.

"What's your hurry, Kaitlin? We're just trying to be friendly." Their voices were sarcastic, and I knew they were being anything but friendly. The jerks. Why was this school so damn big? My classroom seemed miles away. I was no longer the cowering newcomer they saw on the first day of school—one more word and I was going to turn around and deck them both. I turned the corner at the cafeteria and heard them laughing behind me.

"Hey, Buzz, maybe we just got the wrong person. Who is that in front of us? Kaitlin Hampton or Kaitlin *Malone*?"

An instant, sickening flash pulsed out to every inch of my body. I stopped. The Bookends came up on either side of me.

"That got her attention, didn't it, J. B.?"

They stepped closer and I moved away, but the cafeteria wall stopped me. I was trapped. Buzz leaned close with his hand against the bricks behind me. "That's right, Kait, we know your little secret. Some of us are smarter than you think and can put two and two together. It's a good thing none of your rich little friends are in your AP classes with you. I guess if you're rich, you don't have to be smart." He leaned closer to my face, and I could feel his hot breath on my skin. The adrenaline burned in my veins and my knees throbbed.

J. B. closed in, both of their faces just inches from mine. "Pretty good game you got going. No way you could have hooked your rich boyfriend if he knew who you really were, right?"

"I don't know what you're—"

"*Shhh.* Don't worry." Buzz reached out and pushed a strand of my hair behind my shoulder. His fingers made my skin crawl.

I flinched away, but J. B.'s arm on the other side stopped me. "Hey, hey, your secret is safe with us. We're friends. Right?"

I didn't answer. I was too terrified to say anything.

"But we know if we keep your little secret, you'll probably want to help us out, too." They finally stepped back, and I took a deep breath. "You do want to help us, don't you, Kaitlin?"

"What do you want?" I asked flatly.

"Not much, considering how much you have to lose. Just a term paper or two," J. B. said. "The midterm is coming up in government. You can manage that, can't you?"

They were crazy! They were blackmailing me! They wanted me to help them cheat on a midterm! What kind of person did they think I was!

I was a liar—I was *that* kind of person—that's what they knew about me. Cheating probably seemed like no big deal, and I knew they wouldn't hesitate to tell Bram if I didn't "help" them. I had no choice. I wanted to tell Bram on *my* timing, not theirs.

"Yes, I can manage that."

"That's what we thought," J. B. said.

Buzz leaned close to me again, pressing me up against the wall. "Oh, and, Kaitlin, just a reminder. Don't *ever* flick my hat again. I don't like that." He seemed like a raging bull in front of me, his nostrils flared, his upper lip lifted in a snarl. My emotions swirled. I didn't know if I was angry, frightened, or maybe both. He finally pushed away from the wall, and he and J. B. walked off laughing.

"Remember, we want A papers," Buzz called over his shoulder.

Right. I glared after them. *This can't be happening to me.* But it was.

I stood there leaning up against the wall for a full five minutes. I didn't want to go back to class and sit in the same room with those slimeballs, but finally a teacher passed by and asked me what I was doing.

"I just came from my senior appointment in the counseling office."

"Well, it looks like it's over, so get back to class."

Everyone seemed like jerks to me today. I was so full of anger and fear, I felt like I was about to pop. I went back to government and avoided eye contact with the biggest jerks of all. My hands were shaking as I tried to take notes, so I forced my mind to think about other things. Maggie Crutchfield. Bram. College. But the anger still simmered.

When the fourth-period bell rang, the Bookends didn't follow me out. I guess they had enough of their sick fun for one day. I hurried to the courtyard for a dose of peace with Bram, but it eluded me. I couldn't focus, and my mind bounced around like an out-of-control yo-yo.

"Gosh, Kait, your face is so hard and tense, I should be chiseling it out of stone instead of drawing it. What's up?" Bram leaned over and ran the stubby end of his pencil down my leg.

I obviously couldn't tell him about the Bookends and the "deal" they had made with me. But there were other thoughts, too, that charged through me like electrical flashes. I blurted out the words before I could even think them through. They came out in one long breath. "What is the unfinished business your uncle mentioned the other night? You seemed upset when he brought it up. Is that what's keeping you from going to college, Bram? Because I saw the counselor this morning, and we were talking about wasted talent and—"

"Hey, hey. Hold on. The unfinished business is just that strip of land I was telling you about. My mom and uncle have figured out a way to get the extra access land they need, once and for all. Neither one will rest until my dad's dream is realized."

"But I thought you said the owners wouldn't sell."

"Well . . . there's ways around that." He looked down at the ground and then off into the distance. I wanted to ask him more, but he went on. "But that's not what's keeping me from studying art." I remembered his argument with his father on the night he died. Did he feel guilty about studying art now?

"Bram, you can't just give up your dream because you blame yourself for your father's death. It was an accident. Just a horrible accident that—"

Bram stood. His face changed. The vein near his temple surged, color rushed across his forehead, and his eyes narrowed to angry slits, their icy blue slicing into me. "Accident? It was *no* accident. My dad was murdered. Pure and simple."

"You sound so hateful, Bram."

"Hate's not a strong enough word for how I feel about the Malones. I hate them all."

He hates them *all*? I couldn't move. For the first time I didn't see Bram but a Crutchfield, and for the briefest moment I could imagine Bram wrapping his Crutchfield hands around my Malone neck and choking out my existence. My childhood fears of the Crutchfields returned, and when Bram reached out for my arm, I pulled away. I had to confront the lie. My father was not a murderer. "How do you know it wasn't an accident, Bram? It could have been."

"There were witnesses, Kait. And they all said the same thing. Garner Malone attacked my dad."

"But he was convicted of manslaughter—at least that's what I read in the papers—that's not murder."

"Manslaughter is just a fancy term for killing someone when you're angry."

Bram was wrong. It wasn't just a fancy term for murder. And it shouldn't have even been manslaughter. I didn't know all of the details of that night, but I knew it was an accident. My father told me. The witnesses lied. The witnesses all worked for the Crutchfields. Couldn't Bram see that?

Bram started to turn away, but then whipped around suddenly. "And what made you think I blamed myself for his death?"

My own tension surged. I wasn't going to back down from his snarl. "That night you said it was your fault because—"

"It was my fault he left so angry, but only one person killed my dad. That stinking bastard killed him—that worthless scumbag—Garner Malone."

What?

What! You don't even know my father . . .

The electrical tension that possessed me flashed down my arm and shot out my hand as I slammed my hand across Bram's face.

We both stood there in horror.

My God! What had I done? The electricity was discharged, and now I felt my knees crumpling beneath me. I hid my face in my hands, not crying but unable to face what had just happened. How could I ever explain this away? How could I explain that the "stinking bastard" was my father? That the "worthless scumbag" was coming home today and would be sleeping under the same roof with me tonight. That a man he so deeply hated was a man I deeply loved.

He would *never* understand.

"I'm going to ask you one more time, Kait. What's up? What's *really* up?" His voice was tense. His anger frightened me. I was going to lose him. I dropped my hands to my lap and looked up to him towering over me. I tried to think of something to tell him, to explain my crazy behavior. A crazy answer popped into my head.

"I'm sorry, Bram. It's just that I got some bad news this morning, and I'm taking it out on you. You see . . . someone close to me is dying. She's losing everything, and so the thought of you just giving it all up—"

I saw his expression change from anger to concern. I sighed with relief. The crazy explanation worked. But then he asked, "Your mother?"

"No."

"Sister?"

"No. Just a close friend." I didn't want to get specific.

"Becky! Oh my God! Is it Becky?" I hesitated for a long time, and he mistook my silence for affirmation. He knelt down and put his arms around me. "Kait, I'm so sorry." He held me close and stroked my hair with his hands. I melted into his arms, forgetting about what we had just said. I wanted to forget everything. I breathed in his touch, his closeness, his forgiveness. "I love you, Kait. The thought of losing you...I can't even think about what Jason is going through."

My eyes shot open and I pushed away. "Jason doesn't know! No one knows! You can't tell anyone, Bram! That's how Becky wants it. Promise me you won't say anything."

He pulled me back into his arms and whispered in my ear. "*Shhh.* Don't worry. I won't say anything. Just let me hold you."

I held on to Bram. I was afraid to let go. How had one little lie grown into a mutant monster? On top of my lie, I was now being blackmailed and Becky was "dying." I thought about the tomato plants in our fields. It was so much work to get them to grow. Cultivation, water, fertilizer, pesticides, and there was still no guarantee we would get the fruit we wanted. My little lie was blossoming by leaps and bounds, it seemed, all on its own.

I had to tell Bram. Soon. He loved me. He said so. But Maggie and Amanda loved each other and look what happened to them. I had read it in Maggie's diaries. When they were younger they had been inseparable, but then their bond had grown into bitter hatred that had lasted for decades. I couldn't let that happen to us. When I was sure . . . when I knew the timing was right . . .

Then I would tell him.

Chapter 17

October 15
I cross a churning black lake with a devouring monster
lurking beneath its surface. There is no time to test the
stones I leap on, but one misstep and I will be food for
the hungry monster. The stones wobble and I prepare to
die, but then I regain my balance. The other side of the
lake seems so far away. So far. How many more stones
until I am there? How many more stones . . .

I CLOSED MY JOURNAL. My analogy of my predicament
wasn't working. I wasn't just the leaper trying to find my
way to safety.

I was the monster, too.

I stretched out across my huge flat rock, my refuge, and imagined Bram's fingers running through my hair, his rich textured voice sharing private thoughts, his eyes intense upon me, drinking in every word I say, and then sharing moments of silence and understanding. Everything about Bram and me seemed so right, but everything about the past could ruin it. I loved Bram's eyes, but I remembered how they had become icy slits that cut into me. It wasn't his fault. He couldn't help how he had been raised.

The Crutchfields and Malones had become like pedigreed dogs, raised and bred over generations for a certain characteristic. Moe, our golden retriever, has never been hunting in his life, but his heritage springs back into action whenever a wayward duck lands in our small reservoir. He slowly stalks, then jumps. Even with Abby and me yelling for him to come back, he still goes after the duck, unable to resist a deeper urge . . . but what about me? Was my need to hate the Crutchfields really gone? Or was I still a slave to engraved urges? I remembered my uncontrollable flash of anger when Bram insulted my father. Could I really let the past stay in the past? I vaguely recalled something a teacher had said in Bible class at Holy Trinity: *Your sins are remembered no more, they are as far as East is from West.* Well, maybe God could forget sins, but he certainly couldn't expect that of the Crutchfields and Malones. My dad would be home in just a few hours' time, and I didn't expect that a year in a prison cell could wipe away the Malone furrow that took generations to cultivate. It would still be there on his face, hidden in his dark eyes, twitching on his cheek...always lurking. He would hate the Crutchfields now more than ever, for separating him from his family for more than a year. No, the sins would not be forgotten.

I heard a rumbling below me and sat up, but it was only Rick's blue pickup truck bouncing up to the Malone Company offices. I lay back down. I only had another half an hour or so until Abby got home. Then I had to go back down to the house to help make my dad's homecoming dinner. After the day's events, I felt like I had no adrenaline left in me, but anticipation of my dad's return still sent flurries skipping through my stomach. He hadn't heard it in my voice, but would he see the lies on my face when he looked at me? I practiced.

"Hi, Dad. I've missed you."

"Dad! I'm so glad you're finally home!"

"Dad, do you know I've fallen in love with a Crutchfield? The son of the man you killed, actually? Did you know the Crutchfields are not the creeps we always thought they were? They're actually quite nice, and I've been schmoozing it up with them for the last month? Maybe we can all get together for a barbecue someday. Can you see all these things on my face, Dad?"

I was nuts. I felt nuts. I hated who I used to be. I hated who I had become.

I sat up and shoved my journal into my backpack and pulled out one of Maggie's. I was beginning to feel that I knew Maggie almost as well as I knew Bram. Sometimes she wrote poetry; sometimes she jotted down events of the day, sometimes just random thoughts—like me. The breeze caught the thin pages as I opened the journal and a small rectangle escaped from the book. I jumped up and chased the paper across the rock, finally grasping it before it flew off the edge. I turned it over in my hand. It was a letter addressed to Amanda Malone. The thin wax seal on the back was still intact and the words "Return to Sender" were scrawled across the front. The letter had never been opened. I wondered if I would be breaking any laws if I opened it now. I carefully slid my fingernail under the wax seal. It crumbled into pieces, falling onto the rock. I pulled the parchment-thin paper from the envelope and read the familiar delicate handwriting. There was no salutation or date—the letter started abruptly.

I have begged your forgiveness once, Amanda. I shall beg it a final time and never again. I shall not bear all the blame for the wrong that has been done. I saw him first. He helped me from the train to the platform and showered me with his attentions. But you were always the prettier one and soon you turned his head. I was happy for you when you were married to Jared, but I always wondered what might have been. Perhaps that is why I allowed his flowery words to seduce me—and it was seduction, Amanda. Do not deceive yourself. Jared used his sweet words to seduce me, just as he uses them to deceive you now.

I shan't make a fuss over the babe's father. In truth I would rather he not know his father to be an adulterer. The shame I lend shall be enough burden for the innocent to bear. Let him think his father to be someone of integrity, not Jared Malone.

But if you shall not forgive me, I at least warn you not to make my life any more unbearable. Stop spreading your evil lies. Bitterness has grown in my heart, too, and I fear the wedge it drives. A final plea, Amanda, a truce, if not restoration.

Maggie

I folded the paper and gently slipped it back into its yellowed envelope. If only they had known...If only they could see how far their hatred had reached. If only Amanda had met Maggie halfway...If only they knew how deeply their lies and betrayals had cut. If only they could have forgotten...

I watched my hands holding the envelope out in front of me, and they slowly began to tear it down the middle. I watched them tear again and again and again, in a frenzy until there were only small pieces slipping through my clenched fists, and then I threw them all up in the air and they flew away on the breeze. And then I heard a voice crying out to the wind, "Damn you, Maggie! Damn you, Amanda! Damn you both!"

Chapter 18

"Do you think he'll look different? Scars or anything?" Abby tried to sound flip as she laid the place mats out on the patio table, but I could hear the fear in her voice. I tried to be patient with her ridiculous questions.

"If he had scars, Mom would have mentioned them."

"She didn't tell him about us going to Twin Oaks High School."

"That's different. She will. She said he talked so much about how everything would be just the same as before— she just couldn't break it to him. So be sure and keep quiet about that—remember, it's Mom's timing."

Abby didn't answer. We went back into the house to get the rest of dinner ready. I chopped lettuce; Abby husked the corn. Everything had to be fresh tonight. My dad said everything he had eaten for the past year tasted like it came out of a can—an old rusty can. He swore he'd never eat canned food again. We were going to barbecue some thick steaks out on the patio. That was the other thing he wanted—to be outside. My mom told me to wait and let my dad pick the tomatoes for the salad—his request, too. He had dreamed of this dinner for so long, he had every detail planned.

At 5:15 the salad was made, minus the tomatoes, the corn was washed and wrapped in foil, the steaks were marinating, the table was set. Abby and I paced around the kitchen.

"Shouldn't they be here by now?" Abby asked.

"Should be," I said. I pulled out a kitchen chair and sat down. I hoped Abby wouldn't go into the thousand and one possibilities of what could have gone wrong. I closed my eyes and could still smell the sweet green aroma of husks and corn silk. Fresh corn. Fresh start. I hoped so.

My eyes shot open when I heard Moe start to bark and whine outside. He only whined for one person. Abby and I were frozen in our spots. We heard the squeak of the screen door but no slam. We both jumped up and ran to the kitchen door and stopped.

Nothing had gone wrong.

He was home. My dad filled the doorway, my mother behind him. There were no scars. No telltale signs that he had been in prison. He looked how he had always looked. Tall with his thick brown hair combed back. His sleeves were rolled up like he had just come in from the fields. There were no changes at all . . . except for maybe his eyes. His eyes looked deeper, darker. He just stared at us like we were part of a dream, and then he lifted his arms and Abby and I ran into them. We held each other and cried. Me, Abby, but especially my dad. He cried and he kissed us, and apologized for crying and then cried some more. My dad never used to cry. I could already see that things were not going to be like they were before.

"I'm sorry," he said. "I've just dreamed about this day for so long. I've missed you girls. You'll never know how much."

I knew. With his arms wrapped around me, I knew more than ever the hole we had had in our lives. We were a family—of four—not three. When we finally let go of one another, my dad looked around the living room like it was the first time he had ever seen it. I watched him walk around touching the coffee table, running his hand along the bookcase, gently patting the top of the television set. Did he have to touch it to be sure it was all real? What horrible nightmare had he lived for the past year? My father did not look like a murderer. I wished Bram could see him now.

He walked out to the kitchen, and we all followed behind him like he was a baby taking his first steps. He stood in the middle of our worn vinyl floor and took a deep breath.

"God, it smells good!"

"What smells good?" my mom asked. Nothing was

cooking yet, and the aroma of the husks had long since wafted away.

"Everything," he answered. "These old wood cupboards. Moe's bowl on the floor. The dish soap. You. I had forgotten all the smells."

My mom smiled and walked over and put her arms around my dad. It was her turn to cry. Abby and I watched as they held each other with their eyes closed. My dad stroked my mom's hair, her sobs muffled against his shoulder. I wished Bram could see this, too. The Malones weren't monsters. We had suffered, too.

"Okay, that's enough now, let's have some smiles and laughter," my dad said when her sobs had quieted. He smiled and held my mom at a distance. "We're a family again. Everything will be just like it was before."

Just like before? Things would never be like before. Not for me. Not for any of us. And not ever, ever again would things be the same for the Crutchfields. Robert Crutchfield would never be returning home.

My mom turned around, smiling and wiping the tears from her cheeks. "Abby, why don't you take your dad out and show him the new kittens in the garage." Miss Kitty, our cat, had rendezvoused with some stray and had three babies. They were just about ready to be on their own. Abby grabbed my dad's hand, and I could hear her pleading with him to keep them all as she dragged him out the door and across the yard.

My mom grabbed the matches out of the drawer to start the barbecue.

"What took you so long?" I asked. "We were starting to get worried."

Even though she should have been happy, my mom still had that worried look on her face that I had become so used to. She brushed her hair away from her face and sighed. "Your father was afraid to come home. We've been driving around for two hours."

"Afraid? Of what?"

"I don't know." She shook her head and looked up at the ceiling. "Maybe that the police would be waiting here for him. Or the farm would look different. Or we would be different...Maybe that you and Abby would feel differently about him." Her eyes shifted from the ceiling to me. "Do you, Kaitlin? Do you feel differently about him?"

I really didn't know, but I knew what she wanted to hear. "No, Mom."

She smiled. "That's what I told him. We just need to give him a little time. It's going to take time for him to settle back in." She turned and went out the back door to light the coals. I watched her from the kitchen window. Soon Abby came bounding up to her with a big grin on her face, her mouth flapping. I couldn't hear the words, but I knew Abby had gotten her way. The kittens—all of them—were staying. My mom wouldn't put up a fuss since my dad had just gotten home, and that was part of Abby's strategy. Miss Kitty already left regular, ungodly presents on our doormat. I couldn't imagine what kind of sick morgue our front porch would become with four cats.

The sun was getting low and an orange haze was

settling across our hills. The rows of tomato plants in the distance became a contrast of deep shadows and bright silver-green crowns. I could see the dark silhouette of my dad walking between them, touching, bending, remembering. I ran out the back door.

"I'm going to go help Dad pick a few tomatoes," I said to my mom and Abby, as I raced past.

"I'll come, too," Abby said.

"No!" I yelled over my shoulder. And for once Abby listened. Did she hear the desperation in my voice? Or did my mother grab her and hold her back? I didn't look back to see. I ran up the hill to my dad.

"Hey," he said, when I stumbled to a stop, out of breath. "Hey."

It was awkward, and I didn't know why. Was it because I had so many secrets . . . or because he did?

"I was hoping you'd come help me like you used to—like before."

We walked down the rows, pointing to one tomato or another. Talking about tomatoes was easier than talking about other things. The season for this field was nearly over and the plants were dry and drooping. This was the small section where we allowed the tomatoes to ripen on the vine. These were the ones we sold at the vegetable stand or used for ourselves. The majority of our tomatoes, those in our north and west fields, were picked green and sold to produce brokers. The tomatoes in our western fields were the ones we were counting on to get us out of debt. The weather conditions on those slopes allowed us to get an unusually late crop, giving us an edge over other growers. My mom made sure we planted every inch of those fields this year—we needed every penny.

My dad pulled a leaf from one of the plants and turned it over. "The plants look good considering how late in the season it is. I guess the new foreman's been keeping a pretty good eye on things?"

"Yeah, I guess so. He seems to know what he's doing. Mom said he noticed some fungus on some plants in the western fields, and he is going to spray as a precaution. I wish José were still here, though."

Our tomato talk was exhausted, and now we just walked silently. I watched his footsteps in front of me. He didn't walk like a murderer, but I couldn't get Bram's words out of my head. *My dad was murdered. Pure and simple.* Bram was wrong, but I had to know. I had to hear it from my dad.

"Dad!" I finally blurted out. He turned around and faced me. "I know you just got home, and I'll never bring this up again. I promise. But I have to know. What happened that night? What happened, *exactly.*"

My dad's eyes looked deeper and darker than they had before. "Kaitlin, I've relived that night over a thousand times in my head, trying to figure out where things went wrong. But reliving that night won't bring back Robert Crutchfield or give me back fifteen months of my life. I told you before, it was an accident. That's all it was."

"Please, Dad, I *need* to know. That's all you've ever told me. That it was an accident. But how?" He stared at me for a long time and I imagined he could smell the Crutchfield scent on me or see the betrayal on my face. He finally turned away and started speaking.

"It was pouring rain that night. There I was, just me and Crutchfield...with his cronies standing behind him in the headlights of the bulldozers. Everything was so loud. I remember that. The rain slapping on the mud. The roar of the bulldozers. And me and Crutchfield soaking wet and yelling above it all. I was telling him they were trespassing and to get off our land. He wouldn't budge. He was just screaming and screaming. Over and over again in my face, and then he came at me. Both of his hands landed flat on my chest, and I reached back and swung. It happened so fast. But then the rest seemed so slow. I watched him go flying back, and even with all the noise of the rain and bulldozers, I could hear the thud. It was a sick, dull sound like hitting a hard cantaloupe with a hammer, and I knew the minute I heard it that he was dead. A sharp rock had sliced into his head and he was gone instantly."

I felt sick, like I had just witnessed the whole thing myself. I pictured Bram's thick blond hair covered with mud and blood, his beautiful blue eyes closed forever, and I understood Allison Crutchfield's loss. I understood Bram's anger, also—to lose your father so quickly, so senselessly—but it was still an accident. I grabbed my dad's elbow so he had to turn and face me. "But if he attacked you first, you were just defending yourself. Why did they charge you with manslaughter?"

"*Involuntary* manslaughter," he corrected. "It shouldn't have even been that, but the only witnesses were Crutchfields or well-paid Crutchfield employees, and they all swore that Robert Crutchfield was just trying to reason with me when I went berserk and attacked him. They all lied, and I had no one to back up my story."

"There were other Crutchfields there?"

"Yes, his brother."

His brother? Bram's uncle Jack? He was so nice... friendly. *He* had lied? I couldn't believe it. But then, that was the Crutchfield legacy. "*Jack* Crutchfield?" I asked.

"That's right." He looked at me strangely, and I knew I had said more than I should. I wondered if at this very moment he was reading all the lies on my face—if he was figuring it all out, one guilty look at a time—but then his smile returned. "But that's all behind us now. In the past. Everything is going to be just like it was before."

I wondered what that meant.

We picked the tomatoes for the salad and walked back to the house. I chopped them up, my mom put the steaks on, and soon we were all sitting down together for the first time in over a year. We held hands and prayed first. We prayed for the crops. We prayed for Abby's soccer game on Sunday; we prayed for one another and for our health. We prayed for everything.

But as always.

As before.

We didn't pray for the Crutchfields. We never prayed for them.

I knew what "before" meant.

Chapter 19

October 17

*Truth. Balled tightly in my fist. A secret. Forever a se-
cret that I can't share. Caught in the middle and I don't
dare open my palm for all to see. The truth is ugly, they
think. The lies are comfortable. It is what they all want.
Who am I to think differently? Who am I at all?*

*I wish I could fling the truth into the deepest part of
the sea, lost . . . gone. But I know one day . . . one day as
I walked along the seashore, it would reach out and
swirl around my ankles, pulling me in until I drowned
along with it.*

"Bitch!"

I looked up from my seat on the patio to see Abby

glaring at me. I closed my journal. Her eyes frightened me. They were cold and black. I looked from her eyes to her hand at her side. Her fingers clutched a book. Maggie's diary. My chest felt like a giant claw was squeezing it. I glanced around to see if my parents were nearby, then jumped from my seat toward her.

"Where did you get—"

"Shut up! Just shut up! You make me sick!"

"Abby, you don't understand..." I grabbed the diary from her hand and tried to turn the conversation around. "What the hell were you doing in my bedroom? Under my bed?"

Abby didn't hear a word I said. She continued to seethe. "I thought you were screwing around with a Crutchfield, but I didn't know for sure until I saw that." She pointed to the diary in my hand. Her face was hard, filled with contempt. I didn't say anything, but Abby went on, snapping her words out coldly, one by one. "You're a traitor, Kaitlin...a filthy slut just like Maggie...I *hate* you."

More than any of her other words, Abby's last words took my breath away, like a hard punch into my gut. We were sisters. We had always fought, but we had never said we *hated* each other. I didn't want her to hate me. Over the last few weeks, I had learned what hate could become. I learned what could become of sisters.

"Abby, please—" I felt my eyes sting.

"Abby?" My mother called from the house. "Did you find Kaitlin's old shin guards? We've got to get going. Your dad's out in the car already."

"Got 'em! Be right there," Abby yelled back.

She looked back at me. "It's sick, ya know. You're related. You guys could have kids with two heads."

"Abby, it's so far back that we're related..." But I knew it was useless to even try and explain. I had to find out something even more important. "What about Mom and Dad? Are you going—"

"To tell? Ha! I have better plans for you, Kait. You're gonna pay, but I'm not going to drag Mom and Dad into this—at least not yet. It would hurt them too much." Her lip lifted into a snarl and her eyes narrowed to black slits. "You didn't think of *that,* did you?"

But I had thought of it. I had thought of it a hundred times. I didn't want to hurt them, but I loved Bram. I loved the enemy. I loved everything about him. His uneven earlobes, the sadness in his eyes, his shy, hesitant smile, the scent of his skin, his silent telling moments when he holds me so close, the taste of his mouth on mine, his voice, warm and soft, saying my name. I loved his name: *Bram, Bram Crutchfield.* I couldn't explain it, but I didn't just love who he was, I loved *what* he was—a Crutchfield. Loving a Crutchfield, in some perverse way, brought me freedom. "Abby," I whispered, "isn't there ever a time we can forgive...and forget?" I held my breath, hoping, waiting for a crack in the hard facade of Abby's angry face. Finally her eyes returned to ovals, her lips relaxed, and her face held no emotion. It was more frightening than her twisted, angry face.

"Never," she whispered back.

ABBY LEFT FOR HER soccer game with my parents, and I was left with a throbbing headache. What did she mean, I was going to pay? Was she going to blackmail me, too? Was I going to be writing her term papers and doing her chores? And did she really mean it when she said she hated me?

I popped two aspirin in my mouth and washed them down with some milk. It seemed I was living on aspirin these days. I had to tell Bram. Today was as good a day as any. It was the only way out of this mess...but then he might hate me, too.

"Damn you, Maggie and Amanda!" Damn my whole line of ancestors who couldn't forget. I grabbed my keys and purse and drove to Becky's. Bram was picking me up. We were going to pick up some sandwiches at a deli and go to the silly little strip of land his family called the "farm." He wanted me to see it before it was bulldozed over. I couldn't tell him that would never happen, though, because short of losing our own farm, there was nothing that would ever make us sell them the access land they needed.

As always, I arrived at Becky's house early to avoid arriving at the same time as Bram. When I walked up to the porch, I noticed there was a small envelope taped to the front door with my name on it. I rang the bell and opened the envelope while I waited.

Dear Kait,
I'm not home. Had to run out. I'm very "sick," you see—at least that is what Jason tells me. But you

probably know all about that, right? Maybe you can catch me at the hospital later, huh?

Beck

I sighed and sat down on the front porch. Becky knew, and she was pissed. I meant to tell her about her "illness," but I just hadn't had a chance. I didn't think Bram would spill the beans that fast. *Oh, Kaitlin, you're screwing up with everyone.*

I'd make it up to Becky somehow. She'd understand. She couldn't stay mad for too long. And she certainly couldn't *hate* me . . . could she?

Chapter 20

My sigh changed to a smile when Bram turned into the driveway. He had an amazing power to make me forget about everything but him. I jumped up from the porch and ran to his car. I slid in next to him and lifted my lips to his. He loved me. I could taste it in his mouth. I could feel it in his touch. Could knowing the truth change that?

"Missed you. Your dad get home okay from his business trip?" Bram asked.

"Oh, yeah. Sorry I couldn't get together yesterday, but my mom had this family thing planned." I had told Bram my dad was just getting home from a long business trip, which was why I couldn't see him on Friday or Saturday.

"Do I ever get to meet them?"

"Sorry, Bram. My parents are both workaholics. They're hardly ever home. But I'll talk to them and see when they'll both be around so you can meet them. Maybe next week." *Yeah. Right. And pigs will fly.* But that excuse would hold him off for a while.

"Well, don't make it next Friday. Don't forget, my mom is planning my big eighteenth birthday bash. She's going all out. Live band and all. But the best gift will be having you there with me." He kissed me again, and then put his Jeep into reverse. "We have to stop by my house on the way—that okay? When I was leaving, Hortensia offered to pack us a lunch, and no way was I going to turn down one of her sandwiches. I didn't want to be late picking you up, so I told her we'd swing by after I got you. It'll just take me a second to run in and grab it."

"No problem. It's nice of her to make us lunch." The truth was, I didn't care where we spent our time together—on the farm, in his car, wherever—just so we were together. The thought of telling him the truth was making me less nauseous now. I was confident that he cared about me in the truest, deepest way. He was always so open and honest with me. It was time that I was the same with him.

"I'm glad we'll have some time alone today, Bram— time to talk," I said.

It was only a ten-minute drive from Becky's to Bram's. Bram stopped his car on his circular drive and hopped out. "I'll just be a second." He ran through the front door. It wasn't until I leaned my head back against the headrest that I noticed a blue pickup truck parked near the driveway that led to the garages. I could only see the back half of it, but it looked familiar. Too familiar. My heart thumped in my chest. Soon I could hear voices, and the side arbor gate opened. I pushed on the lever and leaned my seat back farther so I would be less conspicuous in Bram's car.

Bram's mother walked through the gate first. I held my breath. A second face appeared. It was Rick. Our foreman! What was *he* doing here? I prayed they wouldn't look over toward Bram's car. I slouched lower but never took my eyes off either one. They talked, Rick nodded his head several times, and then Bram's mother smiled. She handed him a large white envelope, and they shook hands. Rick nodded again to something she said and then got into his truck. Allison Crutchfield stared at him as he drove away, a sad, bitter smile on her face, and I stared at her, barely breathing. My eyes were still frozen on her as she walked back through the gate.

"Hey!"

I jumped what felt like three feet, expecting to hit my head on the roof of the car. "God, Bram! You startled me!"

"What are you doing down there?" he asked. "Taking a nap? Was I gone that long?"

I returned my seat to its upright position. "Just relaxing." I felt like I was hyperventilating, and I could hear my heart pounding in my ears. *Slow down, Kaitlin. Slow down.* "Just relaxing and enjoying the scenery. I see your mom had some company. Who was that in the blue pickup? A friend?"

Bram frowned. "Yeah, sort of. Just someone she is doing a little business with."

I couldn't imagine any kind of business Rick could offer to Bram's mother. The only thing he seemed to know anything about was farming, and the Crutchfields didn't farm. "Oh? What kind of business?"

Bram tweaked his head to the side and studied me. His cheek twitched and one corner of his mouth pulled down into a frown—an odd, yet familiar frown. He finally shrugged his shoulders and answered. "Heck, I don't know. Nothing important. Let's go."

But he did know. I could tell. And it was important. I was certain of it. Important enough that Bram would lie to me. Why? We rode in silence to the farm—another clue that Bram was uneasy about what I had seen. His Jeep jostled down the narrow dirt road that bordered our land. I noted the occasional decaying wood posts with broken bits of rusted barbed wire still clinging to them— memorials to an ancient feud. The tiny, winding road led to the old farmhouse and the strip of farm just beyond it. I guessed it couldn't have amounted to more than a hundred acres. The old farmhouse sparkled with a fresh coat of paint. It was surrounded by a little Victorian picket fence and newly planted flower gardens. All quaint, lovely, and perfect—like everything the Crutchfields had. Our old farmhouse and its constant state of disrepair would probably make Allison Crutchfield gag with disgust. Bram drove past the house and up the hill to the last bit of open acreage the Crutchfields could claim. He stopped the car at the crest and we got out.

"Beautiful, isn't it?"

"Yes," I said. I couldn't think of anything else to say. It was more than beautiful. It was breathtaking. And not just the view that looked out to the ocean. I turned around, drinking it all in. Looking back toward the valley of Twin Oaks, it looked like a postcard. A flowing patchwork of homes, parks, trees, with the San Luis Creek winding through it all. Why didn't I see the concrete anymore? I felt a chill, and in the eighty-degree heat I knew it could only be the ghost of Maggie Crutchfield. The entire world had closed in on her, and this was all that was left. Maggie had cared. Why else would she have made sure this last corner of Crutchfield land was preserved as an inheritance? I closed my eyes. I could see how Amanda and Jared had backed her into a corner—this corner.

"I'm sorry, Maggie," I whispered.

"What?"

"Oh, I just meant that I'm sorry we never came here before. It *is* beautiful."

"I have the key to the farmhouse, too. I'll take you inside later, but first I thought we could eat lunch out here." He grabbed our lunch and a big thick quilt from the back of the Jeep, and we spread it out on a grassy knoll that looked out on the Pacific Ocean in one direction and the valley of Twin Oaks in another. Bram finished his avocado-and-turkey sandwich in a few large bites while I had just nibbled one corner of mine. He intently watched me take another bite.

"Forget it," I said. "Hortensia's sandwiches are delicious, and I'm not sharing a single bit of it!" I took a big bite so he'd know I meant business.

He laughed and reached in the bag and pulled out another sandwich. "There's plenty more. That's not why I was staring at you."

"Then why?"

"Just planning my next drawing of you. There always seems to be . . . There's something I'm just not getting. A side of you I think I'm getting, but when I put it down— it's just not there. You're a tough subject, Kait."

"Maybe you just missed the big zit on my chin," I joked. But I knew what he was getting at. Deceit shows itself one way or another. You can cover it up, put a smile on it, but it eventually oozes out like a festering sore. A twitch, a glance, a shrug turning away the truth.

I carefully changed the subject.

"Maybe going to art school would help you to understand your art better. Have you thought any more about studying art in college?"

Instead of answering me, he chomped on his sandwich and shrugged. Bram knew how to avoid the truth, too. I knew he wanted to study art more than anything in the world, but he avoided the subject like a bad haircut. I wasn't going to let him off that easy. His art was too important to shrug aside.

"Well?" I asked again.

He swallowed his mouthful and turned the question on me. "At least I'm going to college. What about you? I know how much you love to write. You're always putting something in that journal, and Josh loves the stories you wrote for him. You have a gift, too, Kait—don't you want to go to college?"

"I don't have to go to college to write, Bram. I told you I am going into my family's business, and I can always write in my spare time."

Bram grunted. "Right. We know how spare time goes. Besides, you didn't answer my question." He grabbed my hand so I had to look at him. "Do you *want* to go to college?"

I tried to shake off the hollow ache growing inside me. I hated the question. I didn't want to think about it, but Bram was making me. I had never even allowed myself to dream about the possibility—at least not until I had read Maggie's diaries. One day I came across a poem that made me sink to my knees on my bedroom floor. She had written it when she was quite young, maybe my age—before the scandal that changed her life forever. They were words from a different Maggie, happy, cheerful...hopeful. One who was not yet consumed with regret and bitterness. I read the words over and over again, until they were written in my heart. I knew how she felt, and at the same time I felt loss at the forgotten legacy. A legacy that could have been. Her words still cut into me. What could have been...

On Being a Writer
Breaking dawn, sweet majesty
Twas ne'er a more glorious morn,

My pen will not let memory fade
The wonder of a new day born.

Letters dance across the page,
Sweet words, orange and pinkish hue,
Joyful in their Godly praise,
Sunrise becomes a brilliant blue.

And tho' I thank the Creator,
For all creation I see,
My heart delights in none greater,
Than the pen He gave to me.

. . . what could have been.

I looked up at Bram. He was still waiting for an answer. I pulled my hand away and stood up. "No," I said.

"Liar. I can see it all over your face. You want it so bad you can taste it."

The ache that started in my stomach moved to my throat. I swallowed hard. Damn his artist's eye! I turned and looked out at the sweeping view of the Pacific Ocean. "Please, Bram. I'm sorry I brought it up. I know college is a painful subject for you, too. Let's forget about it, okay?" I turned back around and faced him. "Let's just enjoy our time together right now. Please."

Bram nodded. He stood and put his arms around me. We held each other, swaying with the breeze, a dance of sorts, to music only we could hear. I felt all of Bram's heartache, and I know he felt mine. We danced to the rhythm of our heartbeats, the waving grasses adding their song, the wispy clouds overhead, our canopy. On top of the crest, the whole world was our audience, and yet we were blissfully alone.

We didn't bring up college again. We finished our lunch and then took a tour of the farmhouse, the inside—of course—as perfect as the outside. Later, Bram sketched a zillionth picture of me, and then we laughed at a curious squirrel digging through our empty lunch sack. Bram finally chased it away and we lay silently on the blanket, soaking in the warmth of the afternoon sun. It was a perfect day, but as we got ready to go I remembered what I was going back to. An angry sister and best friend. I threw the folded blanket onto the backseat of the Jeep. Bram came around to my side of the car and put his arms around me. "I've always wanted to bring you here. I knew you would love it. Thanks for coming with me." His hands ran down my spine, pulling me closer to him. We kissed, and standing on top of the crest, the world seemed perfect, Bram was perfect . . . I could forget about everything . . .

Almost.

I pulled away. I had to tell him. "Bram, I need to talk to you." I looked into his eyes, but instead of seeing the clear blue irises that melted my insides, for just an instant, I saw the flash of Rick's blue truck. My confession lurched to the back of my mind as I thought about Rick and Allison talking, exchanging an envelope, and then Bram's denial that he knew what was going on.

Something was . . . wrong. Something didn't add up. It was a vague, nagging feeling I didn't understand. I couldn't ask Bram. I remembered his frown and hesitation when I questioned him about Rick. What was going on? Surely Allison wasn't dating Rick. It was too bizarre to think about. But what was their connection? What kind of business did they have with each other? I didn't feel good about it. Rick knew how we hated the Crutchfields. Why would he have anything to do with them?

No . . . I didn't feel good about this at all. But I didn't know why.

"Kait? What is it?"

"I need to know what to wear on Friday. Is it dressy?"

Bram laughed. "You'll look beautiful no matter what you wear, but, yeah, I guess it's dressy. My mom bought a new sparkly dress, and she has me wearing slacks and some designer shirt she got. Women really get into that stuff, don't they?"

"Some do. Not me. But I'll make sure I look okay for your party."

"You'll look more than okay. I know that for sure." He pulled me close again and whispered in my ear. "I love you, Kait."

I closed my eyes, trying to get rid of the image of Rick's blue truck. The blue became the ocean, swirling around my ankles. I squeezed my eyes tighter. "I love you, too."

Chapter 21

I WATCHED MR. GREER'S lips move, but none of his words were reaching me. His voice was a distant drone. I didn't care right now about horizontal tangents or differential functions—in fact, he could have been revealing all the details about his "secret" affair with Mrs. Mathis, the PE teacher, and I wouldn't have heard. I had more important things on my mind. Abby didn't speak to me in the car on the way to school. I still didn't know what evil things she was planning as payback for my betrayal. And then the Bookends had intercepted me before school to remind me about the term papers. They wanted them tomorrow so they could look them over before they handed them in on Wednesday. I assured the dirtbags that the papers would be ready. But mostly I kept thinking about Rick, wondering what he was doing at the Crutchfields'. Of course, I couldn't ask him because then he would wonder why *I* was there. I was puzzled, too, about Bram's odd frown when I asked him about Rick... an odd uncomfortable frown I had seen before... *but when?*

"Miss Hampton? Miss Hampton!"

I jumped, and my eyes focused on Mr. Greer. "I'm sorry, I was thinking about something else."

"Obviously. Why don't you file your dreamy thoughts of the weekend under unfinished business for now and join us?"

The whole class laughed, and I felt my face burn. I knew it was about three shades of crimson, making me even more embarrassed. I correctly solved two problems in a row, which made Mr. Greer lay off me. His attentions were directed to new victims.

I couldn't help myself. I drifted back to my thoughts, but now I had a new one. Mr. Greer had unwittingly answered one of my questions, too. I remembered the first time I had seen Bram's odd frown—the night his uncle had mentioned "unfinished business." Unfinished business... the plan to get the access land they needed... a plan I had secretly laughed at. Could Rick somehow be a part of the "unfinished business"? But even Rick couldn't convince us to sell that land. It still didn't make sense—unless Rick was up to something else.

The bell rang, and I went through my other classes in the same distant haze. The complications in my life, of my own making, were going to take a toll on my school-work soon if I didn't come clean, but it was just so hard. I had so much to lose, and I was certain I would lose something. Bram hated the Malones. My parents hated the Crutchfields. And I was caught in the middle, a traitor to both.

After school I stopped by the library to research some things on the Internet that I needed for the Bookends' term papers. I was going to make them good all right. The best. They would never blackmail me again. From the library I went to the Malone Company offices. I had to type my term paper—and the Bookends' papers—on the company computer, but I also wanted to do some snooping around. I guess my latent Malone loyalties were finally kicking in, and I was in defense mode. Something wasn't right, and I wanted to find out what "it" was.

I parked my car outside the offices and walked in.

"Mother McCree! It's hot in here!" My dad wiped his forehead and switched the fan on his desk to high. The metal Quonset offices were in their "bake mode," as we called it. We joked that anyone who worked in the Malone Company offices always came out well-done—one of the fringe benefits.

"Oh, it's not so bad, Dad. You should have been here a few weeks ago, when it was really hot."

My dad looked down and rubbed the palm of his hand with his thumb, like he was trying to erase something—a new habit I noticed he had developed. "You're right. I should have been here," he said.

He was right. He should have been here . . . everything always seemed to come back to the Crutchfields. They *had* lied. My dad told me so. But I didn't mean to remind him about his absence, and I was glad when he forgot about his palm and started shuffling papers on his desk.

"Yup! As soon as we get the check from that big fat contract your mom landed, the first thing we are going to do is buy an air conditioner for this office—and the second thing we're going to do is get you and your sister back in Holy Trinity."

I looked down at my feet. I didn't want to talk about our old school.

My mom had spilled the beans about Twin Oaks this morning as Abby and I were getting ready. It was like it exploded out of her—she couldn't keep the secret any longer.

"Garner, the girls don't go to Holy Trinity anymore. There was just no money, and the school had already let them go for free the last half of the previous year. They were sorry, but they couldn't afford to carry us any longer."

My sister and I stood at the top of the stairs, watching. It felt like all the air in the house had been sucked out. We couldn't breathe.

"Well . . . ," my dad asked slowly, "where do they go then?" His eyes narrowed like he was bracing himself for the answer.

I could have measured the time in centuries as we all stood there waiting for my mom to answer.

"Twin Oaks," she whispered.

Another airless century passed. My dad was silent, his eyes narrowed farther, but the turmoil he was trying so hard to contain finally escaped.

He slammed his open hand against the wall. It was his first taste that maybe things couldn't be as they were "before." Then his shoulders slumped, and he just shook his head and walked out the back door.

"Go ahead, girls," my mom called up to us. "Finish getting ready. It'll be okay." She left and followed my dad out the door. My eyes narrowed with the same bitterness as my father's had just moments ago...I hated the Crutch—

No! No. I didn't hate them. I hated everything that was happening. I hated the pain my parents felt. I hated myself for being such a coward, such a liar. I hated a century of lies...I hated that a forgotten legacy was slipping from my grasp...but I didn't hate *them*.

Now as I watched my dad shuffle papers and rub the palms of his hands, I wanted him to know that everything didn't have to be as it was before.

"Twin Oaks isn't so bad, Dad. Traditions change. We survive." I shrugged, trying to seem casual.

He looked up at me like I had just spit in his face.

"No, Kaitlin. We have traditions *to* survive. Don't forget that."

I had no intention of going back to Holy Trinity— ever. I had a new life that included Bram, and not even my dad could change that. "But Dad, Mom said the money from that contract is to pay off our tax bill. She said she can hold the lawyers off, but the IRS won't wait any longer. It's the money or our land."

"We're going to pay off our tax bill, but there will still be a little left over to get you and your sister back in Holy Trinity for a few months, and after that—we'll come up with something. We always do."

Our eyes were locked. I saw a man, a boy, a baby so indoctrinated in a lie, in a history of hate, that I only felt sorry for him. It was no use. I went over and plopped my books down on my mom's desk. I remembered my main purpose in coming. "Mom's done a good job, hasn't she? Especially getting that contract with Coast Produce, huh?"

My dad smiled. "Yes. She is amazing."

I casually flipped open my folder and pretended to be looking for something. "And what about Rick . . . What do you think of him?"

"Kind of a strange fellow. Doesn't say much, but he seems to be on top of things. He's out getting the strawberry fields prepped for planting right now, and he's applying pesticide to the tomatoes in the western field on Thursday. He's going to nip that fungus in the bud."

"Everything else . . . in order around here?" I asked.

My dad stood and started toward the door. "Far as I can tell. But then again, I'm just getting used to being able to walk through a door without getting someone's permission." He looked back at his palm and erased away something else with his thumb. "It will be a while, I suppose, before my mind is really back on the business. Any reason for asking?"

"No reason." I pulled a paper from my folder and pretended to be reading it. I couldn't arouse suspicion. I couldn't let on that I had seen Rick at the Crutchfield house, or I would have to explain why I was there.

My dad pushed open the door. "I'm going back down to the house. You staying?"

I nodded. "Yeah, I have some school stuff I need to type on the computer."

As soon as my dad left, I closed my folder and walked around the partition to Rick's office. I looked at his cluttered desk filled with empty soda cans, crumpled papers, and a stinking ashtray. I had no idea what I was looking for, but I opened a drawer. Rubber bands, scraps of paper, stubby pencils, pliers, plastic spoons, loose bits of twine—junk. Nothing that hinted of some diabolical plot. I closed the desk drawer and opened the file cabinet next to the desk. It contained ordering records for the last four years. I recognized José's neat handwriting from prior years at the top of the manila folders, and Rick's slanted scrawl on the past year's records. There were separate folders for everything from fertilizer, to pesticides, to plastic sheeting, to wooden stakes. But nothing diabolical there, either. I guess I was hoping I would see something obvious, like a folder labeled "Crutchfield." I thumbed through the folders anyway. Nothing unusual, but I noticed that Rick had recently changed vendors on the pesticides. I studied the most recent invoice. He had ordered from VegPro and not Mason's Farm Supply as José had always done. Why? I looked back at one of José's old invoices. Rick had ordered a different pesticide, aldicarb, but it was also cheaper than what José had ordered. I guess I should really commend Rick for being thrifty. I closed the file drawer and bent down and opened the one below it.

"Whatcha lookin' for, girl?"

I jumped and stumbled against the cabinet. Rick was leaning against the partition. My spine felt like it was dribbling down to my feet. "Well?" he asked again.

I forced air into my lungs. "I was looking for a pencil. Mine broke."

Rick walked over to his desk and pulled a pencil from a cup sitting on top, loaded with various pens and pencils. He held it out to me. "Like this?"

I shut the file cabinet and tried to laugh. "Sometimes it's hardest to see things when they're staring you right in the face. Thanks." I grabbed the pencil and went back into my mom's office. I knew Rick watched every step as I left. It was only a partition that separated the offices, so I could hear him shuffling around and opening drawers. I knew he couldn't possibly have that much office work to do, and yet he stayed the whole time I was there. Shuffling, moving his chair around on the gritty floor, clearing his gravelly throat—but I was certain he was not working.

I took my time on the term papers, still hoping that Rick would leave, but he didn't. I gave the completed assignments I did for the Bookends a final once-over on the computer screen. The assignment: "Thoroughly research and describe the actions of a political figure in American history whom you admire and who could serve as a role model for today's civil servants. Minimum 1,500 words." I had carefully chosen the political figures for the Bookends' papers—ones I knew our teacher would be familiar with—and I had more than met the minimum required words. I knew the twits would be happy. If they only knew...

I printed them out and began work on my own paper. It was nearly dark when I finished, and I packed up my work and left. When I got home, I looked back up at the company offices. The windows were dark.

Now that I was gone, Rick was, too.

Chapter 22

"AWESOME. Senator Robert Taft." Buzz nodded his head as he flipped through the pages. "This is way more than fifteen hundred words. Why did you write so much?"

I tried to hide my disgust at Buzz's slimy grin. "I just wanted to make sure you were happy."

"This seems like it's good. Really good. But who is Representative George Norris? I never heard of him," J. B. said, as he looked at his own paper.

"Trust me. He's somebody. They're both men of integrity and *courage*. Something we all probably need a little more of." I turned and walked away. It was risky leaving the papers with those two slimeballs. I had a lot riding on timing, and I prayed it would work in my favor, but it was something I had to do.

"Hey, Kaitlin!" Buzz called after me. "Good work, but if you really want to make me happy..." He made some vulgar sounds, and I could hear him and J. B. laughing their warped laughs.

I shivered. I felt like I needed a bath as I took my seat in biology. I sat at the black lab table, blinking my eyes, trying to follow Mr. Shidrowski's scrawls on the chalkboard. I forced my hand to take notes. Systemic poisoning. Toxins. Residue.

Later in my government class, it was impossible to concentrate. With the blackmailing slugs sitting so smugly just feet away, I couldn't hear a word of Mr. Bailey's lecture. I slipped my journal in my textbook so Mr. Bailey couldn't see and lost myself in that world instead.

I read through past entries and felt a closeness to Maggie, feeling the same sadness, fear, maybe even hopelessness that I saw in her diaries. Even the hatred. But I didn't want to follow in Maggie's footsteps—entirely. I didn't want to be consumed by this madness that seemed to thrive in Malone and Crutchfield blood alike. I had seen a glimpse of a hopeful, happier Maggie. That's the part I wanted to carry on.

I jotted in my journal so it looked like I was taking notes.

October 19
Two figures dance, alone on top of a hill. Their dance, a story about how far East really is from West. When sins are remembered no more. When each day is fresh,

and a smile speaks of a future. Their dance is light, their rhythm joyful, their love more real than the soft grass they tread on . . . and that is enough.

The bell rang and I closed my journal. Joy. The legacy that could have been.

When I got to the courtyard, Bram wasn't there. I sat down on the brick planter and looked at the sky. The wispy clouds of autumn were growing thicker. The weather was still warm, but a cool breeze passed now and then, warning that a new season was on its way. A colder season. The chill blew against my neck and I shivered, but then I saw Bram approaching and I felt a tingling warmth. Would I ever tire of his smile? Would the flip-flops in my stomach ever stop when I looked into his crystal blue eyes? I didn't think so.

"Hey," he said, before he cupped my chin in his hand and kissed me.

"Hey," I said, smiling. *Yup, master of words, Kaitlin.* "What took you so long?" I asked.

"I had to go out to my car to get something." He sat down next to me and grabbed my hand. "For you," he added. He let go of my hand and reached into his jeans. "Sorry, it's not in a fancy box or anything." He pulled a small yellow envelope out of his pocket. "But this is what the jeweler put it in."

I was confused. I didn't know what a jeweler would put in an envelope, or what Bram could have for me. "What . . . I don't—"

"It was Maggie's," Bram said, as he ripped open the envelope. "I found it in the bottom of the trunk. I asked my mom, and she said I could give it to you—since you're so interested in Maggie's diaries and all. The clasp was broken so I took it to a jeweler, and he fixed it and cleaned it up." He emptied the envelope into his palm, and then held out each end of a gold bracelet, the small links meeting in the middle to hold a tiny gold heart.

"Bram..." I shook my head. I couldn't accept a gold bracelet, especially not a family heirloom...but then again, I *was* family. I held my wrist out. "Bram, are you sure?"

He leaned over and pressed his mouth to mine. "I'm sure." He snapped the clasp shut, and we both stared at the circle of gold around my wrist. "I want you to wear it on Friday to my party, okay? I want the whole world to know how I feel about you."

I slid my arms around him and closed my eyes. "I'll never take it off, Bram. I want everyone to know how I feel about you, too." I wanted it so badly that the truth seemed like it was about to tumble off my tongue.

"My whole family will be there on Friday," Bram went on. "Even my uncle Jack is flying in from Las Vegas, but he doesn't need a bracelet to know how I feel about you."

"I guess it's going to be quite the party for your uncle to fly in."

"Well, he has some business to take care of, too, but, yeah, it's going to be a great party."

The scent of Bram's skin, the feel of the bracelet

dangling on my wrist, Bram's hands running down my back, all of the seductions that I wanted to give in to ... still, for a moment, were pushed aside. I had to ask. I slid my hand along Bram's chest and down across his thigh. His breathing was heavy. "Is the business with that access land that you mentioned still going on?"

"Yeah," he said, between kisses, "but it's just about finished. Uncle Jack says that land is as good as ours now. We'll finally be able to build the retreat my dad had planned."

My guilt surged. Because of my deception, I was learning things I had no right to know. But what did I really know? Just that the Crutchfields were working on some business deals. It wasn't a crime to try to get land, and they had always done that. I was ruining a special moment with Bram by thinking about bitter, ugly things. *I won't dwell on it! I won't be like Maggie or Amanda!* But what did he mean that the *land is as good as ours now* ... Had they finally beaten the Malones? Did they finally find a way to rip away our greatest source of pride—the undivided Malone acreage? Impossible. They couldn't do it.

I wouldn't think about it anymore. I would only dwell on joyful things, like Bram whispering into my ear, the tiny gold heart pressed against my skin, the party on Friday night, and the fun I would have dancing with Bram. I wouldn't think about Crutchfields, Malones, and their dirty business again. Only the joy. Joy and a legacy that could have been. That could still be.

After school I stopped by Mrs. Flannery's office.

"What can I do for you, Kaitlin?"

"I wanted to see if I could get those applications you talked about—just to look at them. That's all. Just to see what they're like. Is that okay?"

Mrs. Flannery nodded her head. "Of course. It's always a good idea to look things over—just in case." She pulled some papers out of files and printed others out on her computer and slipped them all into a packet for me. "Here's applications for admissions and scholarships. If you need any help filling anything out, come and see me. I'd be happy to write a letter of recommendation for you, too."

"Thanks, Mrs. Flannery, but like I said, I'm just looking them over."

"Of course, dear."

I stuffed the packet in my backpack. My vision became blurry as my lower lids filled, and, strangely, I didn't think of the tears as my own. They were a gentle nudge, the sound of a long-held breath, a sigh of a dream forgotten. Tears held back for more than a century. Maggie's tears, that perhaps a dream was remembered.

Chapter 23

IN BETWEEN TAKING NOTES in biology, I absently fingered the gold heart on my wrist. It would go perfectly with Becky's red winter formal dress from last year, if she would let me wear it. She hadn't returned my phone calls. I called her again as soon as I got home from school to tell her about the bracelet and, again, she "wasn't home." But I knew Becky would forgive me once she made me squirm a little, which, of course, I deserved. In fact, for all my lies, I deserved a lot more than a little squirming.

But mostly I thought about the party, and I played it out over and over again in my head. Bram would hold my hand all evening. Everyone would admire the gold bracelet on my wrist and wonder what it meant. We would dance and laugh and everyone would think we were the perfect couple, and they would be right. We were. But I also kept seeing Uncle Jack flying all the way from Las Vegas to come to Bram's party. Then I would see a white envelope, a blue truck, and Allison Crutchfield's sad, bitter smile. And instead of hearing Mr. Shidrowski drone on and on again about toxic residues, I heard Bram saying, "That land is as good as ours."

He sounded so sure.

I looked at the clock.

That land is as good as ours.

Six more minutes.

That land is as good as ours.

The hands seemed frozen at six minutes till eleven.

That land is as good as ours.

It was only review for a quiz and I already understood about...

Oh my God.

The blue truck swirled in front of my eyes, then a pink invoice, and then a field of ripening fruit. "Oh, my God!" I said out loud. The sounds, the shuffling in the classroom seemed to echo and everything became black around me, a confusion of mismatched noises as I desperately tried to read again the words on the pink invoice. *Alsi—no, aldi— aldi-something—think, Kaitlin! Think! Aldi—aldi—carb! That was it, aldicarb!*

I scooped up my folder and backpack and ran from the classroom. I had to go use the library computer to research aldicarb—*now*. I could hear Mr. Shidrowski calling after me. "Kaitlin! The bell hasn't rung! Class isn't over!"

But he was wrong. Class was over. The whole day was over for me.

Chapter 24

CRUMPLED SHEETS OF PAPER were still clutched in my hand as I steered the car to a stop in front of the Malone Company offices. I felt every drop of the Malone blood raging through my veins as I slammed the car door shut behind me. I burst through the front door and was only vaguely aware of my mom and dad seated at their desks. They said something to me, but I couldn't make out what it was—my ears pounded with the same wild beat that was driving me like a madwoman into Rick's office.

He was leaning back in his chair, his feet up on his desk. He looked up at me. I could feel my nostrils flaring as I took a deep breath to speak.

"You're fired, Rick! Get off our land!"

He smirked, like he was amused at a little child's tantrum.

The fire that burned inside of me exploded, and in two angry steps I was across the room, kicking his chair so his feet went flying off his desk. "You heard me! Get off our land!"

"Now you just wait a minute, missy. I don't work for you, and you can't—"

"That's right! You don't work for me—you work for the Crutchfields. You're so far in their hip pocket you can't breathe! How much did they pay you, Rick? Was it worth it?"

Rick stood up and smiled, his eyes darting nervously back and forth between my mom and dad, who were now on either side of me. He rubbed his bristly chin. "Now this is just plain crazy talk."

"Kaitlin!" my mom gasped. "What on earth are you—"

"There's nothing crazy about this." I stepped forward and threw the crumpled papers in my hand into Rick's face. "Aldicarb! Read it, Rick!" I yelled. "But I guess you already know, don't you! Heck, you've got a hundred freakin' cartons of it in the storage shed!"

"Now let me explain about that—"

"You don't need to explain," I yelled. "I know what's going on. That's why you switched vendors, isn't it? The old supplier never would have sold you aldicarb, knowing what we grow. Aldicarb isn't registered for use on tomatoes. It's toxic—*highly* toxic. One application and our field would have been ruined—our *name* would have been ruined! No one would touch anything grown on Malone land again!"

Rick pointed his long callused finger at me. "Now I've had just about enough of this, young lady. I knew about the aldicarb. They gave me the wrong stuff, and I was going to take it back and—"

"When, Rick?" My dad took a step closer to him. "You had the fields scheduled for spiking tomorrow. Just *when* were you going to take it back?"

Rick swallowed and tried to smile again. "Now, you're not going to listen to the wild imagination of a seventeen-year-old, are you?"

My dad looked at me, his eyes silently searching mine, like he had always done since I was a little girl. I wondered if he could see anything besides rage. He turned back to Rick. "You heard her, Rick. She said you're fired. She's a Malone, the same as us. Pack your things and get out."

Rick looked to my mom, but she only nodded agreement.

He snatched his keys from his desk and shook his head. "There's nothin' here I want to take with me, you ungrateful—" He stormed toward the door but stopped in the doorway and glared at me a final time. "You're crazy, girl, and your big lies are going to get you in a lot of trouble."

I glared back. A liar, maybe, but not crazy.

I continued to stare at the door long after Rick stomped off, listening to the last faint rumblings of his truck roaring down the hill . . . knowing I had thwarted the latest episode of revenge. Was it our turn now?

I felt a safeness that the Malones would survive another day, but I also felt an emptiness, like I had personally reached in and ripped out a piece of my own heart—a piece of Bram's heart.

Your sins are remembered no more, they are as far as East is from West . . .

East and West still glared eye to eye in Twin Oaks.

My nails were still digging into my palms, the furrow on my brow, deep, when I finally realized someone was saying my name.

"Kaitlin? Kaitlin?"

I turned around. My mom's eyes looked frightened, like she was uncertain what had really happened in the last ten minutes. A hurricane named Kaitlin had blown in and fired someone she had trusted. But my dad's face was blank, like he wasn't quite sure who he was looking at. "How did you know?" he finally asked.

I could have lied. I could have said any number of things. I was getting good at quick comebacks.

I could have.

"It doesn't matter," I said flatly. "I just knew." I turned and walked out, and my parents didn't stop me. I suppose it was something in my voice. I could hear it, too. Like I was teetering on a ledge . . . or maybe I had already jumped off.

I knew it wouldn't end there. They would want more answers eventually, but I spent the afternoon up on my rock, trying to return to something I was when I was ten years old, and my parents spent the afternoon being what they had always been. I saw them drive out to the storage shed, and a while later a truck from VegPro arrived. Boxes were checked against invoices, until most certainly, every box of aldicarb was accounted for. And just as certainly, I knew they plotted a way to make the Crutchfields pay. Amanda and Jared would be proud.

I watched it all from my rock and imagined the same frenzy that was going on at the Crutchfield household. So many things to decide. Would Rick still get all of his money since the plan failed? How did the Malones find out? Could it pass as an honest mistake? What shall we do next?

The VegPro truck finally left at dusk. I hugged my rock a few minutes longer, wondering if Bram knew that the "unfinished business" was still unfinished... and did he care? I rubbed my cheek against the gold bracelet on my wrist, pressing the tiny heart to my skin.

"I had every right to fire Rick," I said aloud. "I did. It doesn't matter how I found out. It was wrong. What they were planning was wrong." I remembered kissing Bram, running my hands along his chest, his thigh, and then asking about the unfinished business. "I had every right." I jumped up from my rock and started toward home. I wasn't ten, and sitting on a rock in the dark wouldn't change that.

Abby was waiting for me when I walked in the door. She was standing at the bottom of the stairs. "I hear your boyfriend is trying to poison us."

I looked around to see if my parents were within earshot. "Well, you heard wrong," I said. I tried to push past her to go up the stairs, but she moved over to block my way.

"I just wanted to let you know that I need you to work my shift for me on Saturday."

I laughed. "Right. I don't think so."

I tried to get past her again, but she grabbed my arm. She glanced toward the kitchen and lowered her voice to a whisper. "You don't get it. I'm not asking you—I'm telling you." I finally got her point. Payback time had begun.

I wanted to be angry, to be hateful. I wanted to be hateful enough to scratch my nails across the face of a blackmailer. I searched for it, but the hate wasn't there. Instead when I looked at Abby, I just saw someone tangled in the same sticky web as me.

I shook my head. "I'm not working for you, Abby, but you do what you have to do." I pulled my arm free and pushed past her.

"I'll tell," she yelled up to me.

I hesitated for a moment on the stairs, then continued toward my room.

"Then you'll tell," I called back.

Chapter 25

October 20

How many faces does regret have? The quiet face of a lie, barely whispered. The seductive face of prying questions. The shrewd face of a deception well planned. The longing face of a dream never realized. How many faces . . . too many to count, and when I look in the mirror, I see them all.

I LEANED OVER THE EDGE of my bed and pulled out one of Maggie's diaries. I remembered an entry of hers, not that different from my own. Perhaps the saddest entry I had read in her diaries. I read it again.

Regret

If my tears could wash away deceptions,
Then the very world would be clean,
If regret could make right my wrongs,
The rightness of the whole world would be seen.

But alas, wishes cannot make things a'right
Regret can only unfold,
A path I shall not take again,
A future I shan't hold.

Sins that cannot be undone,
Follies that age and grow,
The deathly heartbeat of my lie,
Is the punishment I will know.

But those whom I have sinned against,
Evil plans against me vow,
With wicked pleasure, Revenge licks her lips,
Two souls she has captured now.

I fell back on my bed and stared up at my water-stained ceiling, the yellow stains spreading out like bony fingers, pointing at me, saying, "Ha! You're a Malone! You proved it this afternoon."

I was a Malone. I loved my family. I loved our farm—the spiked rows of red tomatoes in the summer and the tufted rows of strawberries in the spring. I loved the musty smell of the earth when it was turned in the autumn, and the peaceful, orange sunsets I watched from my rock. But I also loved Bram. Could I love both? Could a *Malone* love both?

Regret. I closed my eyes, trying to blot out the accusing fingers pointing down at me. It wasn't just two souls that were captured anymore—it was a downright brawl. But I didn't have to be dragged into it. Did I? The facts were simple. My father had killed Bram's father, but it *was* an accident, perpetuated by a legacy Maggie and Amanda would never have wanted or dreamed of. But it could stop—it *had* to stop somewhere. It could stop with me. The truth will be hard for Bram to accept, but he will accept it. Bram is different—I've always known that. And he loves me.

I picked up my pen again.

Regret has many faces, and I have seen them all, but perhaps a new face can be worn by a silly scribbler of dreams.

I closed my journal and slid it into my backpack and pulled out the packet Mrs. Flannery had given me. I opened it up and began filling out the first sheet. Kaitlin Malone. Age, seventeen. Maybe I was a dreamer. Maybe not.

"Kaitlin! Dinner!"

I jumped at Abby's whining scream. My temples throbbed. I didn't want to face my parents at dinner. Not because I was afraid of the truth, but because I knew they were. "Before" was so much easier.

I joined them in the kitchen, putting plates on the table, folding napkins. The conversation seemed to whirl around me, and no one noticed that I didn't join in.

"I think we should sue. Think of all the money we could get."

"Better than sue, maybe we can send one of *them* to jail. It would serve them right."

"Yeah, let them see what jail's like."

"We can't prove they paid Rick to do it."

"Well, he didn't really do anything anyway. Just almost."

"Too close for me."

"We need to let those Crutchfields know they can't walk all over the Malones."

"How do we know the Crutchfields were behind it?"

"The Crutchfields are always behind it."

"It's the way they are. They're scum. Some things never change. Let's eat."

We sat down at the kitchen table. I stared at the old blue place mats. I looked at our white plates with small blue flowers bordering the edges. The table wobbled as it always had. The kitchen faucet dripped. We held hands.

"Kaitlin, it's your turn to say grace."

We bowed our heads.

Everything was as "before." Everything.

Almost.

Our heads remained bowed, but no words came out of my mouth. My mom prompted me again. "Kaitlin?"

"Dear God...we thank you for this food. We thank you for our health. We thank you for...your grace." I squeezed my eyes tighter, trying to reach past the familiar kitchen into my soul. "We are thankful for your forgiveness and that in your sight our sins are as far as East is from West . . . and we pray that you would fill our hearts with that same grace toward our enemies." I gripped my mom's and my sister's hands tighter. "We especially pray for . . . the Crutchfields, that you would heal their pain and help us to reach out to them with the same grace that you give to—"

My mother jerked her hand away. I opened my eyes and saw that everyone else's eyes were open, staring at me, disbelief in their faces.

My mother stood up, her chair screeching behind her. "Their pain? Their pain! What are you talking about?"

"I'm not talking, Mom. I'm praying. You said it was my turn."

"You don't need to pray for the Crutchfields and their pain," she snapped. "The Crutchfields only know about giving pain—not feeling it!"

"But—"

"But what? The pain is *ours,* Kaitlin—not theirs. Mine. And I won't have their name brought to our dinner table."

"They come to the table with us every night, Mom— every night—just not in our prayers. But their pain—"

"That's enough, Kaitlin! I don't know what's gotten into you, but I don't want to hear another word about the Crutchfields' pain. I'm the one who had to watch my husband carted off to prison in handcuffs. I'm the one who had to visit him in jail and tell him everything was fine when it wasn't. I'm the one who had to run a farm single-handed until I thought I would drop. I'm the one who had to worry every day about losing it all because of their vicious lies. I'm the one who had to sleep alone for over a year, and every night wonder if my husband would survive another day in prison. *That's* pain, Kaitlin."

"I know, Mom. It was hard not having Dad here for so long . . . but their dad is *never* coming home. They will always have that pain. It will never go away. So I think they know about pain, too."

My mom stared at me, her rage so numbing her mouth was frozen open. I glanced at Abby. Her face was pinched in horror, and I finally turned to my dad. His lips were parted, a furrow just beginning to deepen across his forehead. He spoke slowly, like his mind was racing way ahead of his words.

"How did you know, Kaitlin? About Rick . . . It wasn't the pink invoice, was it?"

I shook my head. "No."

He didn't seem surprised. He just sat there, silently, waiting for me to go on.

"I saw Rick at the Crutchfields' house. I'm dating Bram Crutchfield."

No one moved. No one seemed to take a breath.

"We're in love," I added.

Abby lowered her face into her hands. My mom backed up, bumping into the kitchen counter behind her. She was shaking her head back and forth. "Who are you? I don't even know who you are."

"I'm a Malone, Mom, just like you—with Crutchfield blood running through my veins—just like Dad."

My dad's chair screeched behind him, and he was around the table in one step, grabbing my arm and jerking me to my feet.

"I don't know what's been going on while I was away, but I'll tell you right now—it's going to stop!"

Even though my dad was trembling with anger, I wasn't afraid. It was such a relief to get a small dose of truth out, I had to get the rest out, too. It poured out of me like a flood.

"You can't stop being what you are, Dad. You are a Crutchfield. Your ancestry goes back to Amanda *Crutchfield*. It doesn't do any good to deny it. And the Crutchfields aren't scum, any more than we are. Maggie Crutchfield wasn't a slut—she was pregnant with Jared Malone's baby. He was a cheat. It was all a lie—from the very beginning."

My dad let go of my arm and stepped back, throwing his hands up in front of him, like he was afraid what he might do to me. "I don't know where you're getting all these wild stories, but I know how the Crutchfields have treated us all our lives. That's not a lie! For God's sake, Kaitlin! Their lies are what put me in prison! They hate us!"

"They don't all hate us, Dad. One of them loves me."

"Love?" my mom said, stepping closer to me. Her eyes glistened. "Kaitlin, honey, I don't know what this boy has been filling your head with, but I guarantee he doesn't love you. It just doesn't happen. He's got to be using you. When he found out you were a Malone, he probably—"

"He doesn't know."

"What do you mean?" my dad asked. "He doesn't know you're a *Malone*?"

I shook my head.

"My God, Kaitlin, what have you been doing?" My dad rubbed the sides of his head and walked in confused circles.

"I'm going to tell him. I just—"

My mom started laughing as tears trickled down her cheeks. "And you think he'll still love you when you tell him the truth? When you tell him you're a *Malone*?"

I looked over at Abby. She had scooted over near the doorway, her eyes wide, perhaps afraid that she would be swallowed up in the giant crevice that had torn through our kitchen. It was a crevice so wide I wasn't sure why I should bother answering my mom. I knew she wouldn't hear my answer. My reply would be lost in the great gulf between us. But I had to try. I reached out and grabbed her hand.

"Yes. He *will* still love me. Because he loves me for what I am—not what a name says I am."

Her face grew hard, and she pulled her hand away. "A Malone *is* what you are." She raised her eyebrows so the furrow on her forehead looked like a deep, ugly scar. "And he'll know that, too."

Was the truth really that hard to accept? That there was no "them"? Would it really mean an end to "us" if we believed the Crutchfields to be just as loving, needy, frail—human—as us? And was my mother right? Would Bram only see me as one of "them" once he knew?

I shook my head. "No! You're wrong!" I yelled. "You just don't know!"

My dad, who had been hunched over the kitchen counter, whirled around. "I've had enough, Kaitlin! Whatever nonsense you've been up to—it's stopping right now. Do you hear me?"

My hands relaxed at my sides. My heart stopped beating its mad rhythm, and every muscle in my face seemed to melt away. "I hear you, Dad," I said softly. "And you're absolutely right. The nonsense is stopping tonight."

I turned and walked out of the kitchen. I heard my mom start to follow me and my dad holding her back. "Let her go. I think we all need a little time."

But time was the one thing I no longer needed.

Chapter 26

BRAM WASN'T AT SCHOOL the next day. I was a few minutes late getting to the courtyard because I had stopped by Mrs. Flannery's office to drop off the college application papers. I didn't have a check for the application fee, and I couldn't ask my parents for one. I dumped all of my gathered change and dollar bills on her desk.

"Mrs. Flannery, there is thirty-five dollars there. You can count it. Could you write a check for me? I couldn't ask my parents, but I will be eighteen in March, long before I would be going off to school, so I should be able to do this myself, shouldn't I? That is, if they even accept me—and *if* I really want to go, that is."

Mrs. Flannery smiled. "Take a breath, Kaitlin." She picked up the packet and looked through it. She smiled again. "Yes, Kaitlin. I will write a check. I'll also send some updated transcripts with this. Are you sure your parents don't want to be a part of this? Most parents are thrilled to have their children go to college."

"My family is a little different."

"That's what all of us think—especially when we're teenagers."

"But mine really is."

Mrs. Flannery nodded. "I'll take care of this. It goes off today."

"Thanks." I started to leave, but she called me back.

"One other thing, Kaitlin. Next month we're having the first of our 'Futures' assemblies for seniors. We have a few throughout the year—sort of a way to hold down 'senioritis' and keep students motivated. Once the college applications are off, everyone seems to let down. Anyway, we're having a couple of guest speakers, but we usually start the program with a talk from one of our seniors. Would you be interested in doing that?"

"Me? Get up in front of everybody and talk?"

Mrs. Flannery nodded. She was crazy. She didn't know me too well. I was the blushing queen. "I don't know what I would say."

"Just what the future means to you, or how you plan to reach your goals. Writing seems to be a gift of yours—you could talk about what that means to you. I'm asking you, Kaitlin, because I do think you have something important to share."

I shook my head. "I'm sorry, Mrs. Flannery, but I

can't." My heart speeded up at just the thought of standing in front of seven hundred seniors. "Thanks anyway, and thanks for helping me with those papers."

I rushed to the courtyard, but Bram wasn't there. I waited and waited, but he didn't come. He had never been absent before. Why today, of all days? The truth was stomping in my veins like a racehorse at the gate. It had to get out.

As soon as I got home I called him. He answered on the first ring.

"Are you sitting on top of the phone?" I asked.

"Yup—I've been here all day waiting for you to call."

"Yeah, right. I bet you're sitting at the kitchen counter next to the phone, eating."

"If you know so much, what am I eating?"

"One of Hortensia's sandwiches?"

"Are you watching me through a window or something?"

I laughed. "Why weren't you at school? Are you sick?"

"No, nothing like that. Something happened here yesterday, and my mom was pretty upset. We were up all night talking, so I slept in and just took the day off."

I knew what had happened. I had made it happen. And I wasn't sorry I made it happen...but still, I felt a heavy ache pushing, pressing, wringing the victory I had thought was mine.

"What happened?" I asked, not really wanting to know but feeling I needed to know.

"Oh, the deal is off again on the retreat. The access land thing fell through." I could hear the disappointment in Bram's voice.

"Bram, what is this retreat? Why is it so important?"

Bram's sigh echoed through the phone. "My dad wanted to build a retreat for families of cancer patients. The hospital isn't too far away, and he wanted to build some cottages where people going through treatment could stay. It was important to him because I had a brother who died of leukemia when he was three years old. He remembered how tough it was for families who had to travel a long way and ended up sleeping in waiting rooms."

I closed my eyes and rubbed my forehead with my hand. Why couldn't it have been for another ugly hotel? "There's other land," I said. "Couldn't you build it somewhere else?"

Bram hesitated. I was grateful I couldn't see his face. "Yeah, I guess we could," he finally answered. "But my mom—well, with my dad gone—it was her way of keeping a part of him alive—his dream. That was where he always dreamed of building it. It was her way of holding on. Does that make any sense?"

It made too much sense. "Yes," I whispered.

We were both quiet. Thinking. Our silence, a strange gift of trust.

I looked out the kitchen window and saw my dad in the distance, walking toward the house. Our silent bond was broken. "Is the party still on?" I asked.

"Oh, yeah. Sure. The party is something my mom is

really looking forward to. It'll be good for her, and me, too, so it's definitely still on."

I glanced out the window again. My dad had reached the back garden.

"Would it be okay if I came over for a little while—to talk?"

"I'd love to see you. I really missed you today, but I don't think now would be a very good time, if you know what I mean. My mom's sitting around in her robe. I'm still in my pj's—one of those kind of days. We can talk on the phone, though."

I couldn't tell him over the phone. I had to be with him. To hold his hand. To be there ready to put my arms around him when he said he understood. To brush my lips across his cheek and breathe in his love. "Will you be at school tomorrow?"

"Yeah, sure."

"We can talk then. It's no big deal . . . I love you, Bram."

"I love you, too."

I closed my eyes. My insides vibrated with a thousand lights all flashing on one thing—truth. I needed to get it out. Right now. But it had to be in person. I owed Bram that much. "I'll see you tomorrow," I said.

I would have to hold the truth back for one more day. Just one more day. We said good-bye and I grabbed my keys from the kitchen counter. I had only taken two steps when my dad walked in.

"Where are you going?" he asked. It wasn't a casual question but held all the contempt of an accusation.

"What difference does it make?"

"I told you, Kaitlin, I don't want—"

"Maybe everything isn't about what *you* want, Dad. Why don't you sell the Crutchfields the land *they* want? We don't farm it, and we could use the money."

"We have never sold any of our land, Kaitlin, and we're not going to start now."

"Why not? Maybe now is the perfect time to start. For God's sake, Dad! It's dirt. Dirt! It's not love. It's not truth. It's not God. Would you stop worshiping it and sell the damn acres!"

He looked at me and shook his head. I could see the hurt in his eyes. "I hardly know you anymore. Some things aren't supposed to change, Kaitlin."

I understood his pain. In some ways it was still mine. But now I also knew another pain, and I couldn't ignore it.

"You're right, Dad. Some things aren't supposed to change...but some things are."

I turned and left. I knew without turning around that my dad looked down into his empty palm, and I imagined the guilt he tried to erase away with his thumb.

Chapter 27

I DROVE TO MY "other" house—another loose end I had to tie up. I knocked on the door and Becky's sister let me in. "She's in her room," she said.

I ran up the stairs. Now that I had told my parents the truth, it was like I had to clean every corner of my dirty house. I tapped on Becky's door.

"Come in," she yelled.

She was half dressed, with clothes splattered across her bed, her floor, and around her ankles. It looked like she was being swallowed up in a sea of buttons and rayon. She looked up at me, her eyes wide. "Well! It's about time you showed up! You never know when a sick friend might kick the bucket—or need help with a zipper." She stooped and pulled the circle of blue around her ankles up to her hips. "Does this make me look fat?"

"Then you're not mad?"

"Maybe a smidge, but I'll get over it. So, what do you think of this dress?"

I walked over and put my arms around her and cried.

She pushed me away. "Gosh, do I look that bad? Maybe I'd better go with the red one."

"No!" I said, laughing and crying at the same time. "I want to borrow the red one."

I wiped my wet eyes and grabbed Becky's hand. "I love you, Beck. You're everything a friend should be, and I'm everything one shouldn't."

"Oh, don't be so hard on yourself. You're so gaga over that guy, your brain is like Swiss cheese—your smarts are just whistling out those holes."

"You don't have to make excuses for me, Becky. I'm through making them for myself—and I'm through lying. I told my parents."

"You what?"

We sat down on the floor and I told her everything. Everything I now understood, and everything I didn't. Maggie Crutchfield. Amanda and Jared. Lies that grew out of control. Families that hated each other because of a secret ancient affair. I told her about forgiving and forgetting and how far East is from West. I told her about accidental legacies and forgotten ones. Sometimes I cried, sometimes I laughed, but it all came out in one long, saving breath. I was surfacing from a deep, deep ocean, and the fresh air tasted so sweet. I told her about the pain of missing my dad, the fear of feeling Bram's sorrow, the agony of knowing that the enemies' tears were as wet as my own. Some things Becky had heard before, some things she hadn't, but she didn't interrupt me. She sat and listened to it all, because she knew I needed to say it more than she needed to hear it. I told her about Maggie and my anger, pity, regret, and, finally, the hope she gave me. I was only one person in the large family of Crutchfields and Malones, but I was at least *one* who could pass on a different legacy to my children. I could. I would. No matter what.

I reached over and grabbed Becky's hand. "Don't you think so, Becky? Don't you think I can make a fresh start? Don't you think one person can make a difference?"

Becky smiled and nodded, her blond hair bobbing in her face. "I think you just blew East and West back where they're supposed to be. But what about Bram? Have you told him?"

"Not yet. I wanted to tell him today, but he wasn't at school, and when I wanted to go over to his house, he said it wasn't such a good time. So I'll have to wait till tomorrow at school. I can hardly keep it in anymore. The truth seems so much easier than lying now."

Becky scrunched up her face. "You're going to tell him tomorrow at school?"

"Why? What's wrong with that?"

"Well, tomorrow night's his big party. I know who you are won't make a difference to him, but it will take some time to sink in. And then if he tells his mother—it just might make it kind of awkward. Gosh, you've waited this long, Kait, why don't you tell him after the party, when everyone's gone home. That way he can sleep on it, and tell his mom in the morning."

Of course she was right. Telling the truth would lift a burden from me, but with all of Bram's family there, it would put a damper on the evening for him. The worry and fear I have had would become his. I couldn't just think about what I wanted—what was good for me.

No . . . I'll let him enjoy his party, and when it's over we'll take a walk down to the gazebo and I'll tell him. I will explain it all and he'll understand. In the quiet of the night, when the world is at a distance like the far-off twinkling lights of Twin Oaks, when for that moment our love is all that matters, when we can look into each other's eyes and know that history has nothing to do with us, then I will tell him.

He loves me. He will understand.

It would take time, but one day he would understand, too, that my dad is not a "scumbag." He is just one more person caught up in the web that Amanda and Maggie accidentally wove more than a hundred years ago. My dad is a good man. Bram would see that, too.

"You're right, Becky. I'll tell him after the party."

Becky smiled and nodded, then her eyes shot to my wrist. *"Ahhh!"* she screamed, as she yanked my hand to her lap. "What's that?"

I smiled as I touched the small gold heart held between the smooth links. "A gift from Bram," I said.

Becky rolled her eyes. "I guess this means I'm going to *have* to let you borrow my red dress. It's the only one that will be *too* perfect." She jumped up and pulled me to her closet. "Every eye is going to be on you, girl. I think it's going to be a night you'll never forget!"

I hoped she was right. I hoped it was going to be a new beginning for Bram and me...a new beginning for all the Crutchfields and Malones.

$\mathcal{C}$hapter 28

IT WAS IRONIC that my dad, who was more full-blooded Malone than all of us, took the news of me and Bram best of all. Best, that is, if you consider that he at least still talked to me. My mother, who technically was only a Malone by marriage, had obviously let the Malone legacy creep into every inch of her being. For the first time I wondered about the furrow that ran across her brow. How had she gotten it, too? Not by genetics. Had she always willingly embraced this legacy, or did it invade her gradually like a slow-growing cancer? I don't think it was a matter that she wouldn't speak to me—I think it was more that she couldn't. I wasn't able to see the lump in her throat, but I knew it was there. Her scars from the past year were still too fresh for her to even begin to comprehend that I was forgiving the enemy.

Abby didn't speak much to me, either—just the bare essentials, but it was her looks that I couldn't figure out. Her glances weren't exactly glares. They were blanker but still with the same intensity. Since I had nipped her blackmailing scheme, was she trying to figure out another way to get me to work for her on Saturday?

I was hanging Becky's dress up in my closet when I heard a tap at my door. "Yeah?" I called.

The door opened. Abby stood there and finally whispered, "Dinner's ready."

I felt that familiar knot swell in my throat. Abby never came up the stairs and knocked on my door to announce dinner. She never whispered. I understood why people clung to the past. It was more comfortable. "Before" was so seductive.

I nodded, but she didn't leave. We stood there silently facing each other, and the knot in my throat grew larger. I had turned my whole family's life upside down with just few words—but those words were the truth, and the truth held me as tightly now as my lies had just a few days ago. She finally started nervously twisting the doorknob, and I was grateful for the clicking that severed the silence.

"Something else, Abby?"

She looked down at my worn carpet and ran her toe across an old stain. "No," she said. "Well, maybe just one thing. Was that true what you said about Maggie?"

Maggie. The cornerstone of the Malone hate. "Yes," I said.

She lifted her gaze back up to mine. I still couldn't read the emotion swimming in her eyes as she spoke, but I saw her upper lip lift in a defiant gesture. "If you're such a Crutchfield lover, why did you fire Rick?"

"Loving one doesn't mean I can't love another. I'm still a Malone, Abby. I still care about what happens to our family."

She looked back down. Something else still clawed at her thoughts. Maybe the only thing that really brought her knocking on my door. The nervous clicking of the doorknob stopped. Her lip lifted higher, and she cocked her head like she was desperately clinging to something.

"Last night when you prayed, was that just your way of telling Mom and Dad—or were you really..." Her voice trailed off.

"Praying to God?"

She nodded.

The answer was easy. Truth was easy. "Both," I said.

She tried to manage a last glare at me. "Dinner's ready!" she snapped, and she closed my door behind her.

Chapter 29

Friday, October 22

Free. Flying. Falling. For the first time I feel the wind rushing past my face. I hear the whistle of truth, whispering, "Come, you are free." And I am. Only one weight tugs at me, and I know it will soon be gone, too, and the knowing makes me lighter than air. I can smell, I can see, I can feel without the heavy blanket of fear dulling my touch. I am falling from a ledge, but I am falling up. The truth holds me up. Dusty dreams are reborn, dusty lies die as a scribbler of dreams remembers just how far East is from West. If not for the tug . . . the small, fluttering tug . . . I would be completely free.

"Yes!"

I jumped, Bram's loud shout startling me. "What's the matter?" I asked, closing my journal.

"Nothing's wrong! It's perfect." Bram held up his sketchbook for me to see. "I think I finally got it. You looked so relaxed today, I guess it made me relax, too." He leaned over and kissed me, and we both looked back at his portrait of me.

It was true. I could see what I had been feeling all day. A sense of contentment, knowing all the lies—more than a century of lies—would soon be over. A feeling of peace. Only the small tug—but soon that would be gone, too. Bram was so happy today. I could see the excitement on his face. I couldn't spoil it by giving him something so big to think about, something so big to hide from his family just before his party. My tug would wait.

"So what does your dress look like?" he asked.

"It's gorgeous. That's all I'm going to tell you—except that your eyes better fall out when you see me."

"Never. I don't want to miss a single second of looking at you. Are you sure you don't want me to pick you up?"

"No. You're going to be too busy. I'll drive."

The lunch bell rang. We gathered up our backpacks and stood to leave. Bram wrapped his arms around me and nuzzled his face in my hair, sliding his hands down my back, running his lips across my cheek. "I love you," he whispered. "I can't wait for tonight."

I pushed back and looked into his sky blue eyes. They

were clear and free, the way my own soul was beginning to feel. Only a few more hours...

"I love you, too—and I know tonight will be perfect."

He gave me the portrait to add to my collection and we said good-bye.

THE HOURS THAT passed seemed to go by in a strange rhythm—like a soft, surreal march. At home everyone seemed to move to the same beat. Car doors shut, glasses were emptied from the dishwasher, Moe chased the kittens, and the screen door slammed—all to the same rhythm as if the world knew, even if the people didn't, that something important was about to happen. I pinned all of my portraits, drawn with Bram's sensitive hand, to my walls, no longer hidden beneath my bed, to this same knowing beat. And then when I showered, I allowed the rhythm to wash down my naked body, the soap swirling at my ankles, washing away the fears that lured me into my lies in the first place. *He loves me, he will understand* became a chant that kept time with the beat. I let the steamy air sear away my last doubts.

As I dressed the beat continued—one step coming naturally after another—and before I knew it I was standing before my mirror in Becky's red dress, my hair piled on top of my head, a few stray curls streaming down. Perfect. I hardly recognized the girl in front of me; the one filled with so much hate just a few short weeks ago. Hate for the Crutchfields, hate for Twin Oaks High...maybe hate for the whole world.

I looked at the clock on my dresser. The hands ticked to the same quiet cadence. Seven-fifteen. It was time to go. I didn't understand the strange, calm rhythm, or perhaps it was just a new feel to me—maybe what the truth always felt like. Five steps to my door. Twelve steps down the stairs.

My parents were sitting on the old blue couch in the living room. They looked up at me when I came down the stairs. My dad stood. "Where are you going, Kaitlin?"

I looked into his deep brown eyes—the only thing that had really changed about him since he went to prison. He knew. I could see it in his eyes as surely as he could see the truth in mine.

"You know where. I'm going to Bram's house."

My mother jumped to her feet. "You most certainly are n—"

My dad put his hand out to hold her back. "Please, Rachel," he said. He turned back to me. "It doesn't matter to you that we told you not to see him?"

He knew the answer to that one, too. Why did he make me say it? I ached inside, the gentle rhythm that had guided me shattered. "Before" was calling, beckoning, asking me to ease into its suffocating comfort. But I couldn't go back. The truth slipped from my tongue, and I shook my head. "No. It doesn't matter." I grabbed my keys and left before the image of their pained faces burned into my memory. They would have to work through the truth in their own way—if they even wanted to.

I drove through the streets of Twin Oaks, knowing

that it was the last time I would be driving with this ugly lie inside of me. Soon I would be free. My stomach jumped, the cultivated Malone reaction at the thought of revealing truth—to a *Crutchfield.* "Stop it!" I scolded myself. "He loves you. He's different. He *will* understand." I glanced into my rearview mirror. My makeup, my hair, Becky's dress, the circle of gold dangling from my wrist, everything was perfect. I knew it was an omen. Tonight would be perfect, too. My old Buick may have been closer to a pumpkin than a golden carriage, but I still felt like Cinderella.

I pulled into Bram's long driveway, and as I approached the house, I could see that a throng had already arrived. I parked my car on the outside edge of the circular drive between a sporty Beemer and some hugely expensive car I didn't know the make of but I could tell reeked of money. It had a fancy ornament on the hood and a paint job that looked as soft and smooth as chocolate mousse. I shook my head at my poor, rusty monster sandwiched between the two. "Behave yourself," I said.

The evening was cool with a brisk breeze. Black clouds hovered overhead, and I could hear rumbles in the distance threatening our first storm of the season, but I left my jacket in the car anyway. I didn't want to spoil Bram's first glance at my dress, and I didn't want to hide the bracelet on my wrist. It was only a piece of metal, but to me it was a symbol, a visible thread that connected me to Bram. Proof that we had accomplished what five other generations couldn't. Perhaps my lie wasn't such a bad thing after all. Without it we might never have given each other a chance. "Soon, Maggie," I whispered, "soon it will be over." Maggie and I both let out a deep, relaxed sigh.

The fountain in the center of the drive trickled, and I could see other guests up ahead walking through the front door. Jenny and Matt had finally hooked up and walked hand in hand. Lexie, still shy, arrived with them and hung close to Jenny. I was sure Jenny would do some serious matchmaking tonight, if only to give herself and Matt a little space. A group of five older people, probably friends of Allison's, followed behind them, and I could hear more car doors slamming shut behind me. It looked like it was going to be a huge party. I guess the Crutch-fields never did anything in a small way.

I walked up the steps, Becky's dress feeling like a sensuous hug. I smoothed it out at the top of the stairs and walked through the open front doors. My skin tingled. Hortensia was standing there greeting guests and taking jackets. I handed her my purse and watched a smile spread across her plump brown face as she looked at my hair and dress. "Oh, Kaitlin, you are—beautiful." She raised her eyebrows and nodded her head on the last word, and we both laughed. I knew she remembered what it was like to be seventeen and in love.

I looked around for Bram, but there were so many people milling around in the entrance hall I couldn't see a thing. I smiled and squeezed through the crowd until I reached the living room. A band was set up over near one set of French doors, playing some quiet background music, but Bram had already told me they had the word to let it rip at nine o'clock. I spotted Becky and Jason over near a huge buffet table, piling dainty little plates with hors d'oeuvres. Caterers hovered nearby to fill in holes and clean up spills as they appeared—more of the Crutchfield magic. I expected Bram to be near the food, too, but he wasn't. I smoothed my dress out again and started across the room. Maybe Jason knew where Bram was. I had only taken two steps when I felt like I was being watched. In a room packed with people it was a silly notion, but, still, I knew I felt it. I turned my head back around and caught my breath. Bram's beautiful blue eyes were staring at me, and the look on his face was the one I had dreamed about. He was out on the patio, leaning against the doorjamb, his lips slightly parted, his eyes speaking everything I needed to know. One, two, three seconds, the unbroken gaze continued—the rest of the world fading behind our silent bond.

Guests milled in between us, breaking our eye contact, and we started weaving our way through the crowd toward each other. I felt like I was floating across the polished wood floors. When we reached each other, Bram grabbed my hand and pulled it up to his lips. "I have everything I want for my birthday now," he said. He stepped back and paused. "You're *beautiful*."

We squeezed over near the band, and I laid my head on Bram's shoulder as we danced our first dance, savoring his hand placed snugly against my back, his gentle kisses on my ear, the warmth of our bodies pressed so close together, the hushed comments of nearby dancers saying what a perfect couple we were.

We danced one more dance, and then Bram pulled me around to introduce me to more relatives and old family friends. The party spread out across the whole house and spilled to the outside patios, too. Elegantly decorated buffet tables were in the dining room and halls. Bartenders were set up at one end of the living room and out on the patio. A giant white canopy covered most of the patio as insurance against bad weather, and portable heaters were strategically placed. Besides the caterers, extra help was sprinkled throughout the house, their starched black-and-white uniforms part of the backdrop. Bram seemed completely comfortable with the extravaganza, but it was completely foreign to me. I didn't want to embarrass him, so I tried to act like I had been to parties like this dozens of times before. I smiled and tried to be gracious and poised as he introduced me to more people than I had ever met in one evening. Of course we finally made it over to one of the food tables and Bram refueled. I was still too excited to eat anything. Becky and I talked while Bram and Jason stuffed their faces.

"Doesn't Jason look hot tonight?"

I laughed. Becky was as crazy about Jason as he was about her. "I think you're the one with the raging hormones now."

"Ha! Maybe so. I'm going to take him for a little walk down to the gazebo." She raised her eyebrows. "It is so romantic down there, with all the twinkling lights."

"If it starts raining, you might get stuck down there for a while," I warned her.

Becky raised her eyebrows and smiled. "You're finally catching on, girl." She grabbed Jason's sleeve as he was midgulp and pulled him through the French doors, chatting away about the twinkling lights.

Bram smiled through a full mouth, and I slipped my hand back into his.

Allison finally stepped away from a group she had been chatting with and came over and hugged me. "Kaitlin, you look just beautiful! I think red's your color. Are you having a good time?"

"Perfect. It's a perfect evening and a perfect party." It was truly more wonderful than I had imagined it would be. I smiled and looked at Bram. "And of course I have the perfect date, too."

"I can't disagree with that, though I admit I'm a bit biased." She turned to Bram. Her face nearly glowed as she smiled at him. "How about you, honey? Having a good time?"

"The best," Bram said. "But I think I'm going to have to pull the plug on this music."

"Now, Bram, it's only eight-fifteen. Give us old folks a few more quiet moments before we have to hide out on the patio."

A bright flash, followed by a crack, made us jump. Through the windows I could see little crowns of water splashing up from the pool. "Oh dear, excuse me," Allison said. "I'd better go have Richard check the canopy and make sure there are no leaks." She smiled and hurried away to the patio.

"Now's my chance," Bram said. "Any requests? I'm going to go talk to the band."

I rolled my eyes. "I'm not going to get in the middle of that one. You heard your mom. It's only eight-fifteen."

Bram flashed his beautiful, seductive smile. "Chicken," he said, and leaned over and kissed me. "I'll be right back. Don't go away."

I watched him weave his way through the crowd, occasionally stopping to laugh with a friend or playfully punch one in the arm. I loved everything about Bram and wondered how one person could make me feel so warm and full and right with the world.

"I think I know what he's up to."

I jumped. Uncle Jack had come up on my right and I hadn't noticed. "Sorry, I didn't mean to startle you," he said.

"Oh, that's okay. I was just . . ."

Uncle Jack smiled. "I know. Bram can't keep his eyes off of you, either. You look quite stunning, by the way."

I opened my mouth to say thank you, but suddenly I got a strange feeling, again, like I was being watched. Had I seen something when I whisked my eyes from Bram to Uncle Jack? I looked back toward Bram. He was lost somewhere in the crowd. It couldn't have been him; his stares made me feel warm, not strange. My eyes scanned the room. Past the buffet tables, past the dancing couples, past the band, past the open French doors, and out onto the pat—

My eyes jerked to a halt. Two gray, lifeless eyes were staring back into mine. My knees suddenly felt loose and hot. A burning wave wrenched from my stomach to my chest. The room around me vibrated as I locked onto the gaze, trying to make sense of it. It couldn't be. The eyes smiled, and I felt my last waiting breath escape in a choke. "Oh, my God."

It was Rick.

He gave me a small, barely perceptible nod, like a hyena sizing up its prey. He turned his head. His eyes were now scanning the room. He started moving toward the band. *Oh my God. Oh my God. No.*

Not now.

I gasped in some air and frantically scanned the crowd, too.

"Kait? Kait?" Uncle Jack was grabbing my arm, but I was pulling away. Yanking away. My eyes jumped from Rick to the crowd. We both pushed our way through the wall of faces, searching.

I had to get there first. I had to.

People pushed, held on to me, wanting to talk, dance. "No!" I yelled to the groping hands. I felt like I was drowning in a sea of bodies and I couldn't catch my breath. I could only see Rick's face—getting closer. "Bram!" I called, but I couldn't be heard over the clamor of the party. I pushed and finally stumbled through to the clearing in front of the band. My eyes landed on Rick first, then Bram poised before the microphone. Bram raised an eyebrow and tweaked a sideways smile, confused by the sudden rush.

"Bram! I need to—"

"Well, this is a surprise." Rick's loud, gravelly voice stopped me short. He looked straight at Bram but jerked his head toward me. "I never would have guessed that you'd invite Kaitlin Malone here."

Bram's smile faded, and he put his hand over the microphone. "You got the name wrong, Rick. It's Kait *Hampton*. She's my girlfriend, I ought to know."

The whole room spun around me. Terror choked at my throat. My mouth was open, but no words would come out. My eyes were frozen on Rick's hideous grin.

Not now. Please, not now.

Rick laughed. "Kaitlin Hampton? Is that what she told you? Well, boy, I think you've been had. Looks like the Malones had their own spy snoopin' around here. Bet they've had a good laugh about it, too. Yup, that's Kaitlin Malone, all right."

Bram glared at Rick, and I could see the vein at his temple bulge. "Shut up, Rick. You're drunk. You don't know what you're talking about." His hand had dropped from the microphone, and his words echoed throughout the room. The crowd was instantly quiet.

I forced out a few gasping words. "Can we go outside—"

"I'm not drunk enough that I don't know Kaitlin Malone when I see her. Hell, she's the one who fired me. Musta been wheedlin' things outta you, boy. Yup, looks like you've been pokin' a Malone and didn't even know it."

Bram exploded. He flew at Rick, catching his jacket with one fist and swinging with the other. Uncle Jack,

Matt, and the band members jumped in the scuffle and pulled the two apart. Blood trickled from Bram's lower lip as he pulled against the arms holding him back. "You drunken liar! Get out of my—"

"Now you listen to me, boy. I'm not lying to you." Rick turned and looked at me. "This here's the daughter of the man who murdered your daddy. Ask her. Go ahead, ask her!"

Bram, Uncle Jack, Matt, a hundred eyes turned and rested on me, an ocean of silent, suffocating faces, all waiting. I stared back into the only face that mattered to me. Bram's eyes were expectant, confident. Not a single word slipped from my mouth, but Bram's artist's eye read my face. I watched his raging muscles droop against the arms that held him. The surging color in his face drained. The disbelief crippled his body like a ravaging disease.

"Bram, please." My voice wobbled and I swallowed. I blinked my eyes, trying to clear my vision. "Let me explain—" I took a step toward him.

He jerked his arms away from Matt, who was still holding him. "Let me go." He looked away from me and pulled on his sleeves, trying to smooth out wrinkles that weren't there. He walked toward the front door like I didn't exist.

"Bram, please, you've got to let me explain." I grabbed his arm. He yanked away and pushed through the crowd. I chased after him, reaching, pulling, pleading. The hushed crowd tried to move aside as we stormed through.

"Bram!"

He wouldn't answer me. He burst through the front door, and I followed him, still pulling on his arm to get him to stop.

"Bram! Stop! You've got to listen to me!" I sobbed.

He whipped around on the first step and glared at me. "Listen? To what?" he yelled. "That you've been lying to me, making a fool out of me, and *using* me?"

I grabbed both of his arms, afraid he would turn away again. "I haven't been using you. I swear. And I was going to tell you. Tonight! I was going to tell you tonight!"

Bram twisted his arms away and wiped the blood oozing from his mouth with the back of his hand. He leaned close, his voice trembling with rage. "Tonight? What makes tonight so special? Why not last night? Or the night before? Or the hundred freakin' nights before that? What were you waiting for, Kait? Your family having too much of their sick fun?"

He turned, not waiting for an answer, and stormed down the steps out into the pouring rain. I followed him. I pulled his arm, screaming behind him as he continued to walk. I stumbled as I held on, but I wouldn't let go. "What if I had told you?" I cried. "What chance would you have given me? My father killed your father, and that's all you know—or all you think you know. I wanted you to know *me*, Bram, really know me, and somewhere down the line to know my father. He isn't what you think, Bram. Your father's death was an accident. He fell on a rock. It was just a horrible accident."

Bram stopped abruptly, and I stumbled forward. We were near the back of his Jeep, the rain drenching us both.

He grabbed me by my elbows. His dripping hair fell in front of his face as he looked down at me. His fingers dug into my flesh. His eyes were glassy cold. "Fell?" He pulled me closer, a frightening smile smearing his face. My heart hammered in my chest in one long frenzied beat. "When my dad turned his back, your scumbag father picked up a rock and smashed it into his skull—twice. *Five* witnesses all told it the same way." He pushed me away. "Some accident, huh?"

I couldn't speak. He was wrong. He had to be. I stood in the rain, icy beads pelting my skin. But it was the sting of Bram's words that numbed me. This wasn't how it was supposed to happen. Everything was getting turned, twisted. I was going to tell him when we were alone, when the time was right. He would understand. He was different. We were different. East. West. A new legacy.

I rubbed my pounding head. I couldn't think. *It was an accident. It was a lie. The journals.* I had so much to tell. Explain. My thoughts were trapped in a horrible, tangled web.

The jingle of Bram's keys jolted me back to the driveway. I was running out of time. I was losing him. He opened his door, and I desperately clung to him one more time. "Bram, I love you. Isn't that all that matters? I love you."

He looked at me, and I felt my insides crumpling inward. The pain in his eyes was deeper than any love that had been there. I saw betrayal. Mine.

He shook his head. "I don't think you even know what love is." He got into his car and slammed the door.

"Bram! Bram!" But he ignored my cries and screeched off down the driveway. The wild scream of his tires quickly melted behind the sound of the rain slapping the pavement. I stood there alone, dripping, freezing, Becky's red party dress no longer feeling like a sensuous hug.

This wasn't how it was supposed to happen.

I turned and saw Allison and Uncle Jack standing in the doorway. I walked toward the steps. Maybe. Maybe I could explain to them. I walked up the stairs, leaving a dripping trail behind me. "Mrs. Crutchfield—"

"We welcomed you into our home," she said, shaking her head, disbelief washing over her face. Her eyes glistened with the same painful look of betrayal I had just seen in Bram's. "We trusted you...How could you do this to us...How could you do this to Bram?"

"I didn't mean to—"

"Hortensia!" Allison's face grew rigid. She didn't want answers to her questions, either. "Give Miss *Malone* her things and see that she leaves." She went back inside and Hortensia hurried out with my purse. She slipped it into my hand with a worried look and went back inside and shut the door. In a single breath, I was alone. What happened? Was this all a grisly nightmare?

I turned and walked back to my car. My hot tears were disguised by the rain. Only my shaking shoulders revealed my cries. I fumbled with my keys. None seemed to fit. They were a blur and I couldn't find the right one. *Damn!* They slipped from my grasp and I fell to the pavement with them, doubling over, the rain and thunder muffling my sobs. I couldn't wipe the image of Bram's look of betrayal from my eyes.

"Whose turn is it now?" I cried. "Is it over? Is it over? Is it over?" I sobbed with ragged breaths. I pounded my fists on the wet ground, the words not just my own, but Maggie's choked sobs, too. "Are we even? Is it finally over?"

Never. For Bram, Allison, my parents, Abby—it would never be over.

I pulled myself back up to my door and found the right key. My frozen fingers wrapped around the steering wheel. My sopping dress soaked the seat, red dye running down my legs like blood.

Bram was gone.

The quiet tug I had felt all day, the last lying tug I thought I had under control, had in a hideous instant grown into a devouring monster. It devoured me.

This was not how it was supposed to happen.

Chapter 30

I DON'T REMEMBER driving home. I don't remember getting my car stuck in the mud. And I only vaguely remembered climbing onto my rock in the blackness of the pouring night. The safe blanket of the blackness . . . that I remembered.

The darkness was just lifting when I felt my father shaking me, cursing and afraid, wondering if I was even alive. He carried me to his truck and drove me home. I stared at him as the truck jostled over the rutted road. Would I ever know the truth of that night? Or was the truth a victim of angry, misshapen memories? My father was a good man. I believed that. So was Bram's. Maybe that was the only truth there was. I slipped back into my shivering fog.

My mother stripped my wet clothes off my trembling body and put me in a hot shower, but I continued to shake. I didn't feel cold, only numb. They asked me questions and I opened my mouth, but I wasn't sure what I said. I couldn't hear. The loud rumble of the rain, the thunder, and Bram's stinging words were the only sounds echoing in my ears. They put me to bed, piling blankets on top of me to stop the shaking. They didn't know. The shaking wasn't from the cold. It was from the pain.

I woke up hours later. The first thing I did was call Bram. "He loves me," I whispered to myself. "He won't stay angry. He'll understand." I got his answering machine. "Bram, please, call me. I need to talk to you." I left my number—my real number. I called every fifteen minutes, leaving the same message. After the seventh or eighth time, I only got busy signals. They had taken the phone off the hook.

I lost track of time. I kept reaching back, wondering, searching, trying to remember exactly what happened. Becky called, crying and apologizing for telling me to wait. "It's not your fault, Becky. Timing had nothing to do with it. There never would have been a good time. Some things just never change." My voice was tired and flat.

Becky continued to sob. "I told him the truth, Kait. Everything. The real truth. All about the legacies, the East and West stuff, forgiving and forgetting—everything you told me—but he didn't listen to a word I said. He didn't want to listen." She drew in a long shaky breath. "It's so unfair. You're the one who should be mad after what they tried to do to you."

"It's not just last night, Becky. If he listens to you, his whole life becomes a lie. Who can live with that?"

Becky offered to come over, but I said no, maybe another time. The day continued in a dark, hazy fog. Abby didn't go to soccer. My whole family seemed to be moving quietly around me, going from one useless chore to another, looking at me. I know I looked pitiful. I didn't get dressed or comb my hair. I didn't care. When Abby picked up the phone, I yelled, "No! He might try to call."

But he didn't call. He wasn't going to call. The truth settled in the pit of my stomach like a heavy rock on the bottom of a deep, deep sea. The truth was drowning me. He was a Crutchfield. I was a Malone. Period. Case closed. The phone would not be ringing for me. I sat on our ancient, frayed blue couch and reached up and touched my cheeks. They were wet. When would it stop?

THE NEXT MORNING I moved through the same fog, going through motions, making my bed, straightening my desk, trying to feel the tiniest purpose to my life. I had been wrong about everything. Everything. There was no purpose. I pulled books from my bookcase and dusted the shelf behind. What was important? The dust? The truth? Anything? Drops of water fell on my dirty dust rag. My cheeks were wet again. How could I have been so wrong? Some things never change. Who was I to think they could? Who was I at all? I didn't feel like Kaitlin Malone anymore—at least not the old Kaitlin Malone—and I could never be Kaitlin Hampton again.

I stacked the books back on my shelf. It was clean now. Did it make a difference?

My bedroom door was open and I heard a clanging knock on the screen door. A few seconds later my dad called my name. "Kaitlin? There is someone here to see you." I could hear the strain in his voice. The fog was blown away in one strong gust. *Bram! It had to be!* I flew out my door. I was halfway down the stairs before I focused on the person standing on the other side of the screen door. It was Hortensia. My elation crashed with a horrible thud. My feet were heavy, and I could barely make them move down the rest of the stairs. I felt like I had used up my last scrap of energy. She had the same worried look on her face I had seen at the party. My mom and Abby walked in from the kitchen. Every eye was focused on our visitor.

I pushed open the screen door. "Come in, Hortensia." I searched her face, looking for some flicker of hope, but there was none.

She wrung her hands. "I—you see—" She stumbled over her words and finally blurted out the reason for her visit. "Mrs. Crutchfield sent me. I'm here to get back the diaries she let you borrow. She wants them all returned."

Could anyone feel as empty, as shamed as I did right now? Hortensia's pitiful gaze was a weight I couldn't bear. I swallowed and forced my head to nod. I turned to go back up the stairs to get Maggie's diaries . . . the diaries that led me to the truth in the first place. The diaries that made me understand about accidental legacies. The diaries written by another scribbler of dreams—

I stopped halfway up the stairs, my hand frozen on the railing, my eyes staring blankly at the worn carpeted stair in front of me. A gift, no matter how small or unimportant, had been given to me. Me. A purpose. A legacy no one else embraced.

"Kaitlin?" my mom called, her voice concerned.

I turned around and walked back down to Hortensia. "She can't have them," I said. Hortensia's eyes grew wide. She nervously glanced to the others in the room and then looked back at me. "They're mine," I explained. "Maggie is my aunt, and she left them to me. I know she did. She was—"

"Kaitlin," my dad interrupted. "Maybe it would be best just to give them back."

I shook my head. "No," I said softly. "They *are* mine... but..."

I looked down at the bracelet still dangling from my wrist. I ran my finger along the smooth links and fingered the small heart in the center. My vision blurred as I undid the clasp. "This was a gift—" My voice cracked, and I swallowed, trying to push the stabbing throb from my throat. "This was a gift that I'm sure Bram wants returned." I dropped it into Hortensia's palm. She scrunched her face up and shook her head. I looked into her eyes. I didn't see betrayal, only pain. She understood. She wasn't a Crutchfield or a Malone. She could see beyond the past. I straightened up and took a deep breath. I smiled, for the first time since Friday. Not a full-blown smile that reaches all the way up to the eyes, or into the soul. Just a hint of a smile—not forced, but not effortless, either—the beginning of a smile. A very small beginning. "Mrs. Crutchfield can call me, if she wants me to explain. But the diaries are not leaving this house. Okay, Hortensia?"

She nodded and left. The rest of the evening was silent. The phone didn't ring. Allison Crutchfield didn't call. I knew she wouldn't.

Chapter 31

MONDAY MORNING my parents tried to get me to stay home. "Give it a day or two," they said. "Come down and work with us at the offices or at the vegetable stand." They wanted to ease me back into the comforting cocoon of "us." They didn't say it, but I knew they thought I had learned my lesson about "them."

"I'm going to school," I said firmly.

Before I left I told them about college and new legacies. They needed to know it all. They were angry, disappointed, and certainly schemed after I left to bring me back to my senses. My last act was to give Abby the rusty key ring from my bedpost. I told her it was not my legacy, and maybe not hers, either. She had to choose. She silently accepted it but hid her feelings behind dark, cloudy eyes.

We left early, and Abby didn't balk. As soon as I got to school, I went to Bram's first class. I waited on a bench across from the door, afraid, but still clinging to a small thread of hope. He finally arrived, just before the bell.

"Bram," I called.

He turned and looked at me, his crystal blue eyes penetrating mine, and for the briefest moment I thought I saw into his soul, but then a heavy wall came down. Our gaze continued, one, two, three seconds, but none of the tenderness I craved was there—only cold, detached hate. Crutchfield hate. A sick, warm taste swelled in my mouth. He no longer saw Kaitlin Hampton but Kaitlin Malone, daughter of a Crutchfield killer, a deceiver, a liar.

It didn't matter that the Crutchfields had tried to destroy us by destroying our crop. I had given deception a face. I had made it personal.

I wanted to melt into the pavement below me, my body and all memory of me vanishing from the face of the earth. I couldn't bear to see so much hate in someone I loved so much and know that I had put it there. Bram saved me the trouble of melting. He walked through his classroom door without a word.

"Please, give me a chance," I whispered, but he was gone. I blinked back my tears. When would they stop? I may have embraced my new legacy, but Bram still clung to his old one. He was different ... but maybe not different enough. Could I have been that wrong?

I wrote in my journal during classes and jotted notes in Maggie's. They were truly mine now. The purpose they gave me was the only thing that made me inhale and exhale. Most of Maggie's entries were sad, regretful, bitter, but a few—a very few—showed me something else she could have been, something I could still be. That gave me hope. And small threads of hope were all I had.

At lunchtime I raced to the courtyard. My thread of hope had become frayed and thin, but I still held on. We loved each other. He *couldn't* forget that. I couldn't. And he loved to draw. It was who he was. He couldn't forget that, too, could he?

I waited. He didn't come.

I madly wrote in my journal. It was the hope that kept me going.

THE NEXT DAY I waited outside of Bram's first class again. I promised myself it would be the last time. He glanced at me and walked in, again, without a word. My hand slipped from my frayed thread, and I walked to class. I felt like an empty shell drifting through the hallways. There were no tears left, only disbelief at how stupid I was. If I was wrong about Bram, maybe I was wrong about everything. Maybe I should just go home and work at the vegetable stand. Forget my silly dreams. Embrace my parents and forget about Maggie's stupid journals and all the things I thought I wanted to do. If Bram could forget everything, maybe I should, too. Hate the Crutchfields as we always have. Just go back to "before" and be done with it.

"Shut up!" I said aloud. I was having a pity party, and I didn't really believe a word I had thought. I wanted someone to tell me, "No, Kaitlin, *they're* the ones who are wrong. They're the ones who are blind." I wanted someone to hold me, to believe in me—but there was no one.

No one.

I only had me. It was a bitter, cold feeling. For the first time, I truly understood the frightened, lonely feeling that drove Maggie to sell off the Crutchfield land—her feeble grasp for acceptance. But I didn't have land to trade for acceptance. I had nothing. My empty shell drifted through my classes, torturing myself with thoughts of a sketching hand, a gentle smile, and what should have been.

October 26
Regret is a lonely companion. Its hands are cold. Its words, empty. It whispers what might have been; it taunts me with the foolishness of my lies. So much regret for my lies that hurt him, but there is one lie I will never regret—the lie that allowed me to love him.

Mr. Bailey's voice jerked me back to the classroom. "I have your midterms ready to return to you. Many of you did quite well."

I stuffed my journals away while Mr. Bailey started handing back our papers. These papers were the one other thing I would never regret. He laid my paper on my desk. A large circled A– was at the top. Buzz looked at my paper and smiled. He knew his was better than mine and confidently waited for his A+ paper. Mr. Bailey laid J. B.'s on his desk first, and then tossed Buzz's to him. I watched both of their eyes bug out. A large red F blared across the top of both papers. Their mouths sputtered in disbelief. I could see the spit flying from Buzz's flapping lips.

"Mr. Bailey!" he yelled. "I don't deserve an F! This is a good paper! Really good!"

Mr. Bailey stopped and slowly turned to face Buzz. He smiled. "Yes, Buzz. You're right. It *is* an excellent paper. Better than excellent. Award winning, in fact." He placed his hands on Buzz's desk and leaned into his face. "At least that is what someone thought when they gave John F. Kennedy the Pulitzer prize for writing it nearly fifty years ago. *Profiles in Courage* ring a bell?" Mr. Bailey straightened up. "But maybe I was a bit harsh. Here." He reached over and added a plus sign next to the F. "You did do a very good job of copying it—word for word."

Mr. Bailey turned and continued to hand out papers. Buzz and J. B. sunk down in their chairs. Both of their faces were burning red. Buzz looked over at me and softly mouthed the words "Bitch. You'll be sorry."

I looked away. I wasn't sorry. I would never be sorry.

At the end of class, the Bookends followed me out and repeated their warning. "You're going to be sorry, Kaitlin. Real sorry." They stomped out to the lunch crowd, looking for Bram. When they spotted him standing with Matt and Jason, they turned around to make sure I was watching. If the twits only knew . . .

I could only imagine the words they said to Bram, but even from that distance I saw Bram's reaction. One moment he was chiseled stone and the next he was a swinging lunatic. I'm not sure the Bookends even knew what hit them. Here they thought they were bringing Bram news, when they were really rubbing salt in a seething wound. Matt and Jason joined in the fight. I didn't stick around to see how it turned out, but I knew that even without Matt and Jason, Bram's festering anger alone would have been enough to obliterate the Bookends. The Bookends' plan had backfired, just as mine had.

IN THE DAYS AFTER the free-for-all in the lunch lines, word spread quickly of my betrayal of the Crutchfield "king." I no longer walked down the halls anonymously. I drew stares, whispers, and occasional vulgar titles. A few times I passed Bram in the hallways. Our encounters were silent, but his eyes still made me catch my breath before he looked away. I imagined that I still saw something there, but my lunches remained solitary. It gave me plenty of time to think—and write.

November 4
I am through writing about regret and what might have been. I cannot change the past—only the future. And the only thing I can really change about the future is me. I have me, and I have my writing, two gifts . . . and that is a lot to build a future with. Enough.

I snapped my journal shut. My words *were* my gift. Perhaps the only gift I could share. I went to see Mrs. Flannery. Maybe it wasn't too late.

I asked her if she still wanted me to speak at the assembly tomorrow. She said yes, and though my cowering ego silently shrieked in horror, begging me to run, I told her I would do it.

When I left her office, I saw Bram and the rest of the gang stopped down the hallway, talking and laughing. It was too late to turn around without looking like a complete fool. As I got closer, Jason and Matt looked away. Jenny started searching for some mysterious hidden object in her purse. And Lexie . . . Lexie wasn't shy anymore. She looked at me and then slipped her arm through Bram's. He didn't pull away. My feet stopped moving. I couldn't force them another inch forward. I looked straight into Bram's eyes, wondering if my sin was so great that I deserved this. I'm not sure what he saw when he looked back into my eyes—a mixture of anger, love, my own hurt look of betrayal maybe, but I know his artist's eye captured it. I saw it in his tightened jaw, his deep swallow, the turning of his spirit inward, ashamed.

He loved me. He *still* loved me.

But it wasn't enough, because he loved being a Crutchfield more.

I was wrong. Wrong about everything. Wrong about Bram. About me. I could feel my regret turning to bitterness already. Was hate next? Whatever made me think I could be different from Maggie and Amanda? That Bram could be different from the overbred pedigree that he was? Nothing had changed. Bram would forget his art. I would forget my writing, and we would both melt into the seductive comfort of an old legacy.

I looked away first this time. I felt my eyes burn and my lower lids start to brim with tears that I thought were gone. I still had a trace of pride. I hurried past the group and was grateful that my tears didn't run down my cheeks until they were behind me. I hurried toward the courtyard. I would go and have my miserable lonely lunch, alone, outcast, and forget every silly dream I ever scribbled. Nothing ever changed. Nothing ever would. The heat of bitterness was beginning to warm me. I hated him. I hated the whole world.

When I got to the courtyard, someone was waiting for me. It was Abby. She wanted to have lunch with me. She wanted to keep me company . . . she wanted to *talk.*

I cried. I had almost given in to the past. I had almost run back into the comforting arms of old legacies before I had given new ones a chance to take hold.

THAT NIGHT I worked on my speech, and the next day I found my name being called to talk in front of seven hundred seniors. Even though I had the deepest of motivations, the surest of words, and the spirit of a hopeful ancestor pushing me toward the podium, I suddenly felt like every muscle in my body had turned to overcooked spaghetti.

Am I crazy? Kaitlin Malone isn't a public speaker. Besides, everyone at this school hates me. One of them was born to hate me. What would happen if I just ran away right now? I can't do this! I have never done it before.

And that was the word that slapped me out of my panic. *Before.* Nothing would ever be like before. Not for me. I walked to the podium, my knees shaking, the paper in my trembling hands fluttering like a windblown leaf. No, the old Kaitlin Malone would never have done this.

I searched the sea of faces. They all ebbed and flowed like a wave that was ready to crash over me. If his crystal blue eyes were there, I couldn't see them. The seven hundred faces seemed to grow to a thousand, then to five thousand. It was a growing tidal wave, but I forced my feet to remain planted to the floor. I cleared my throat and tapped the microphone. I didn't even know how to speak into one. I was certified. A lunatic for sure. Just as I had been when I fell in love with Bram. But I didn't regret that—I prayed I wouldn't regret this, either.

"Hel-lo." My cracking voice boomed through the auditorium. I looked down at my shaking paper. The words seemed to shift back and forth across the paper like sand. I closed my eyes. I thought of Bram and everything he could be. This was my last gift to him. He might not love me anymore, but I knew a dream still lived in his heart. If he would listen to me, maybe I could convince him to listen to himself.

I opened my eyes. The crowd had shrunk back to seven hundred. I still couldn't see the crystal blue eyes I spoke to, but as I scanned the faces, I realized the crowd was filled with Brams, Kaitlins, and Abbys. How many of them carried the past with them? How many had legacies of abuse, fear, hopelessness, prejudice, or hate that they would in turn pass on to their children? The past lurked in many of their faces, ready to infect their futures. Maybe this speech wasn't for Bram at all, but for one of them.

I looked back down at my prepared speech.

I swallowed.

I spoke.

"Mrs. Flannery asked me to speak to you today about the future." I looked up from my paper. I didn't need to read the words—they were written in my heart. I looked out across the crowd, frozen and quiet and eager to hear what a liar had to say. But strangely, I suddenly felt calm. How could I be afraid to speak the truth?

"The truth is, the future only lies ahead for a few of us today. For many of us, our future only holds the past. I know. Until a few weeks ago, the past had a choking grip on everything I wanted to be. The past told me who I could be, who I could love . . . and who I should hate. And the funny thing is . . . I never questioned it. I just thought that that was the way it was supposed to be. And then something strange happened. I lied. I became someone else, and by doing that I learned who I *could* be. You see, I thought that by telling a lie, I could change one person, change a whole family, change two families—maybe a whole future—but a lie is never a good foundation for the future. It crumbles when you least expect it. I learned that I can't change people through lies. The truth is I can't change people at all. There is only one thing that I know for sure that I can change—and that's me. A good place to start."

I stepped away from the podium and walked to the edge of the stage. My voice carried throughout the auditorium. "I'm not saying that you should lie to escape your past. Lying has its price, too. I know. But what I am saying is don't let your past strangle you. Will you look back ten, fifteen . . . twenty years from now and regret the person you've become? Will you look back and wonder, what could have been?" *What could have been.* My throat flinched like a fist had just caught me by my vocal cords. I looked down and took a deep breath trying to push away the tightness. I closed my eyes. *Don't stop now, Kaitlin, not now.* I looked back up at the crowd. "If you look back with regret, you have no one to blame but yourself, because legacies don't hold on to you—you hold on to them."

I unfolded the paper in my hands. "I'd like to read something to you written in a diary by my great-aunt over a hundred years ago. She was a woman who lived with regret.

"December 15, 1898
"Oh, to live my life one step ahead of myself—to know the actions that will bring joy or pain. But now Regret holds me in its biting jaws. I feel the teeth sinking in, wishing I could retrace my steps to start my journey afresh, but the teeth sink deeper and my foolish wishes cannot help me escape Regret's bitter hold.

"My great-aunt Maggie made mistakes. She hurt other people, but her biggest mistake was to think she was responsible for the hate that other people loved. We all have the power to move on, maybe even the power to forgive . . . and a few of us, a very few of us might even be able to forget, to put the past as far behind us as East is from West. My great-aunt and great-grandmother couldn't do that and left behind them a bitter legacy. That bitterness has produced fruit for generations—a bitter, deadly fruit. And the saddest thing of all is, it was an accidental legacy, certainly not what they intended to leave as an inheritance.

"So maybe what I am saying to you today is, you all have dreams in your heart—secret, silent dreams that you feel way down in the deepest part of your soul. Don't let mistakes or the legacies of other generations smother your dreams. Go after them . . . because Regret makes a very bitter traveling companion."

I scanned the crowd one last time, but there were no familiar eyes. There was nothing left to say. "Thank you," I whispered.

The silence was overwhelming. Finally a girl in the back row stood and started clapping. It was Abby. I smiled at her through blurry, watery eyes. She had ditched to come see me. Her lonely little clap echoed through the auditorium. Those damn lurking tears spilled down my cheeks, but I guess I really didn't care. If my words made a difference only to her, that was all that mattered. Another girl stood and started clapping, and then a boy, and then a half dozen others. I wondered if Abby had coaxed all of her friends to ditch with her. The rest of the crowd stayed glued to their seats, silent, their arms folded in defiance, forever loyal to their Crutchfield king. But I could see a few shifting uncomfortably, their eyes glazed in thought, the truth settling in the secret hollow of their beings as it had in mine. They knew the pasts they wanted to leave behind. They knew. But it was too hard. Change is always hard.

I made my way down the center aisle searching for Bram—hoping he had come, but I didn't see him. I made a difference to a dozen people I didn't know—but I couldn't make a difference to him. The ragtag applause was bittersweet.

I didn't stay for the rest of the assembly. They would be dismissed for lunch soon, so I went to the courtyard. Abby didn't come. After my speech she told me she was going to the nurse to avoid detention for ditching. Abby was a quick thinker.

I sat down on the brick planter and breathed in deeply. "It's over, Maggie," I whispered. "It's finally over. At least for me." I let out a long sigh, and I knew Maggie sighed with me. So many wasted years . . .

I took out my journal.

I became lost in my words. They lifted me, they guided me, they whispered everything I knew about who I was and who I would become. They brought order out of the chaos, but still they couldn't erase the lingering lump in my throat. If only . . .

"Poetry?"

My head jerked up. Slowly I stood to look into the eyes that reached past my skin—past my name—into my soul. "No," I said, "just thoughts, glimpses, things running through my head."

We stood there without speaking. One, two, three seconds, our gaze continued and neither of us looked away.

Bram finally nodded. His eyes were the ones rimmed with red now. "It's hard to change, Kaitlin...It's so hard..." He looked up like he was searching for more words, but they wouldn't come.

"I know," I said. "Change is always hard." I waited.

He cleared his throat and drew a deep breath. "My family—they're so angry. They're still filled with so much hate. They won't ever—"

"But what about you, Bram? *You.*"

He swallowed, but it couldn't stop the cracking of his voice. "I never did care much for history...and I never—I never stopped loving you."

"Then we're a start, Bram...a good start."

He *was* different.

We were different.

He reached into his pocket and pulled out a thin gold chain with a heart at its center. "I think you dropped this," he said. He fastened it back on my wrist.

I heard the long-held sigh of a century, the dying breaths of Regret, the silent gasp as East lost sight of West, and Bram and I settled down on the grass, he drawing in his sketchbook, while I scribbled dreams of the future...

On a small planet, where minute follows minute, day follows day, year follows year, where tradition marches on with a deafening, orderly beat—sometimes the order is disturbed by a dreamer, an artist, a scribbler—sometimes the beat is changed one person at a time.